British Library V
T0031462

STORIES
FOR
CHRISTMAS
and the
festive season

This anthology first published in 2022 by
The British Library
96 Euston Road
London NW1 2DB

Volume copyright © 2022 The British Library Board
Introduction © 2022 Simon Thomas
For individual copyright notices, see page 206.
Every effort has been made to trace copyright holders and to obtain their
permission for the use of copyright material. The publisher apologises
for any errors or omissions and would be pleased to be notified of any
corrections to be incorporated in reprints and future editions.

Cataloguing in Publication Data
A catalogue record for this publication is available from the British
Library

ISBN 978 0 7123 5452 3
e-ISBN 978 0 7123 6835 3

Series editor Alison Moss
Series consultant Simon Thomas

Text design and typesetting by JCS Publishing Services Ltd
Printed and bound by CPI Group (UK), Croydon, CR0 4YY

MIX
Paper | Supporting
responsible forestry
FSC® C171272

Contents

✻

✳ ✳ ✳

Introduction

✳

What happens in a Christmas story? Some are about the first Christmas, telling the story of the birth of Jesus from a range of perspectives. Some use Christmas as a time of great change – like the transformation of Ebenezer Scrooge in Charles Dickens' *A Christmas Carol*, perhaps the most-remembered Christmas narrative outside of the nativity. Perhaps everyone reading this Introduction will have their own stories of Christmas that are passed down through the years and the generations – the time that a gift was hilariously inappropriate, the meal that went disastrously wrong, the first Christmas in a new home, a new relationship, or with a new baby.

Authors have turned to Christmas as a theme for a story for centuries – whether a momentous Christmas where everything changes, or the documenting of an annual tradition so customary that it feels immovable, bringing either reassurance or claustrophobia. Some of the most respected writers of short stories have used Christmas as a creative spark; equally it has inspired the work of writers whose names have never been widely known, and who never aimed at literary greatness.

✻ ✻ ✻

Stories for Christmas and the Festive Season collects a wide range of creative work by women writing across the twentieth century. It is published as part of the British Library Women Writers series, which brings back and contextualises forgotten or less-remembered novels by female authors, highlighting the realities of women's lives and society's changing attitudes toward female behaviour throughout the decades of that century.

Some of the authors in this anthology (such as Alice Munro and Muriel Spark) are highly regarded and award-winning writers; some are remembered for particular books, but the wider scope of their work has faded from public consciousness. The majority of their stories have been sourced in the British Library collections. We have searched through published collections of stories, delving also into Christmas editions of old magazines. A few of these stories have never been republished since their first appearance in a festive periodical. They sit side by side with much more renowned authors, each giving their own perspective on Christmas.

This anthology is loosely ordered chronologically – not by year of original publication, but by the days of the Christmas period. From early preparations to festivities, on to the pantomime season and ending with a New Year's resolution, these stories take you through the highs, lows and traditions of the festive season.

The anthology opens with 'Turkey Season' (1982) by the Canadian writer and Nobel-prizewinner Alice Munro (1931–). It's an early reminder that Christmas isn't all twinkly lights and beautiful ribbons – because it's told from the perspective of a

❄ ❄ ❄

14-year-old 'turkey gutter' at the Turkey Barn. Or, rather, an older woman reminiscing over being that girl.

> All I could see when I closed my eyes, the first few nights after working there, was turkeys. I saw them hanging upside down, plucked and stiffened, pale and cold, with the heads and necks limp, the eyes and nostrils clotted with dark blood; the remaining bits of feathers—those dark and bloody too— seemed to form a crown. I saw them not with aversion but with a sense of endless work to be done.

Munro has long been one of the world's most respected short-story writers, and you can see why in 'Turkey Season'. It's a portrait of a curious community – people who wouldn't otherwise come together, sharing their lives and keeping their secrets. It's about memory, and the way that it can shift and change over time, never quite landing on certainty. And it shows a side of Christmas that most of us are protected from.

Moving from Canada to Ireland, Maeve Binchy (1939–2012) shows another 'sense of endless work to be done' – but this time in the home. In 'This Year It Will be Different', Ethel is a wife and mother who stages a protest against the festive labour that her family expects she will do alone.

> She didn't do anything dramatic. She didn't do anything at all. She bought no tree, she mended no fairy lights, she sent six cards to people who really needed cards.

❄ ❄ ❄

The story is from the 1990s, but could voice the experience of countless women from any period. Reflections of ordinary life, often in small-town Ireland, run through Binchy's seventeen novels, as well as her short stories and other work. Her debut, *Light a Penny Candle* (1982), sold for the then-largest sum ever paid for a first novel, and remains one of her most popular.

If one isn't on strike, like Ethel, then preparations tend to include Christmas shopping. In a collection of observational sketches called *General Impressions* (1933), E.M. Delafield (1890–1943) included 'General Impressions of a Christmas Shopping Centre'. Though almost a century old, the same dilemmas endure of deciding what to buy for an eccentric uncle, trying to distract fractious children with Santa Claus, and hunting for a gift you *know* you've seen but can remember nothing about. This sketch first appeared in the feminist periodical *Time and Tide*, as did much of Delafield's writing – including her most famous work, *Diary of a Provincial Lady* and its sequels. Her novel *Tension* (1920) appears in the British Library Women Writers series; like 'General Impressions of a Christmas Shopping Centre' and almost everything Delafield wrote, it plays with the idea of self-awareness (and lack of it) and how we might appear to others.

When the shopping is done – or, more likely, in the middle of it – you might find yourself attending a children's Christmas play, pageant or concert. In 'The Christmas Pageant' (1968), by American writer Barbara Robinson (1927–2013), the 'worst children in the world' disrupt a nativity play with their questions and confusion – but end up shining more light on the holy story

＊ ＊ ＊

than anyone expects. Three years after the story appeared in *Woman's Home Journal*, Robinson adapted it into the bestselling children's book *The Best Christmas Pageant Ever*, also published as *The Worst Kids in the World* in the UK. Meanwhile, in Audrey Burton's 'Ticket for a Carol Concert' (1950), everybody has an excuse not to attend the village concert, although they all agree to buy tickets. Burton's story was published in *The Lady* magazine and includes some interesting contextual details. The aptly named Mr Sage can't envisage going to the concert: '"Christmas carols in the year 1950! But just look at the world! Look at it! Look at Korea!"' In every generation, singing about peace on earth can feel like a clash with reality.

For some, Christmas is the perfect time for romance. 'Snow' (1928) by Olive Wadsley (1889–1959) is representative of many stories appearing in women's magazines throughout the twentieth century, and indeed today. There is something comforting about the sudden, headlong infatuation between two young people – simultaneously improbable and inevitable. It helps one agree with the heroine, Viola, that '"Christmas is the loveliest time in all the year"'. Wadsley's romantic novels met a wider audience in six adaptations for silent films between 1918 and 1924.

If the couple stays together, they might form the sort of family traditions seen in Kate Nivison's ''Twas the Night Before Christmas', originally published in *Woman's Weekly* in December 1989. Nivison's story shows a happily married couple, with an undercurrent of intergenerational comparison between mothers and daughters – and a mouse that is definitely 'stirring'.

※ ※ ※

A sudden romance is also at the heart of 'Christmas Fugue' by Muriel Spark (1918–2006), though a rather less conventional one. Cynthia is spending Christmas Day in the air, travelling from Australia to England and thereby artificially extending the day as the hours pass and the time difference catches up. '"Nobody flies on Christmas day [...] It will be amusing," said the pretty hostess. "We'll make it fun."' Like much of Spark's writing, the reader and the character don't quite know where they are – leaving them disoriented. Spark's twenty-two novels enjoyed critical acclaim, with three shortlisted for the Booker Prize, and she is widely regarded as one of the finest writers of the second half of the twentieth century. Her most famous and enduring work, *The Prime of Miss Jean Brodie*, is about an unorthodox teacher in Spark's native Edinburgh. Spark spent relatively little of her life in Scotland, moving between Zimbabwe, London and New York before settling in Italy for the final decades of her life.

Miss Harting, in 'The Little Christmas Tree' by Stella Gibbons (1902–1989), intends to spend Christmas Day alone. She isn't stinting on Christmas food, Christmas decorations and a Christmas tree – even though, in this rural community, 'unmarried females did not buy Christmas trees, decorate them and gloat over them in solitude, however natural such a proceeding might seem in Chelsea'. Some unexpected guests arrive, of course, and the story takes a pleasing turn – though not without ironical touches that devotees of Gibbons' most famous work, *Cold Comfort Farm* (1932), would recognise. 'The

✻ ✻ ✻

Little Christmas Tree' is the opening story from Gibbons' 1940 collection *Christmas at Cold Comfort Farm and other stories*; she would return to the farm again in 1949's *Conference at Cold Comfort Farm*.

Tree in place, it's time to start giving and receiving gifts. The titular present in Richmal Crompton's (1890–1969) 'The Christmas Present' (1922) is an heirloom passed down generations, though an unconventional one. The story shows the wit that Crompton is best remembered for in her stories about William Brown, perpetually aged 11 while appearing in stories published from 1919 to 1970. William and his mischievous, entrepreneurial friends wreak well-meaning havoc on relatives, visitors and domestic staff – particularly any showing signs of pomposity. Alongside the *Just William* stories, Crompton wrote about fifty novels and short-story collections for adults.

"'But what time will your operation be over, mother?'" is the striking opening line of 'Christmas Bread' by Kathleen Norris, published in *Nash's and Pall Mall* magazine in 1924. In 'Christmas Bread', the question is less callous than it might seem – mother is the surgeon, rather than the patient.

"Mother, doesn't it seem funny to you that a patient would have his operation on Christmas Day? Couldn't he have it to-morrow, or wait till Wednesday?"

The doctor's fine mouth twitched at the corners. "Poor fellow, they only get him here to-morrow, Merle. Christmas morning. And they tell me there is no time to lose."

❄ ❄ ❄

While being a female surgeon in 1920s America makes this heroine unusual in one respect, the idea of juggling work and family life around Christmas is as relevant as ever, as are the timeless themes of family feuds and reconciliation.

In 'Christmas in a Bavarian Village', the protagonist is returning to her German home for the first time in many years.

I felt as if I had walked into a Christmas card—glittering snow, steep-roofed old houses, and the complete windlessness, too, of a Christmas card. Not since 1909 had I had a German Christmas, the last of a string of them, and seeing that 1909 is a long while ago, and that many things have happened since, it was odd how much at home I felt, how familiar everything seemed, and how easily this might have been the Christmas, following on in its due order, of 1910.

But this is 1937 – and many things have changed, and are changing, though they lie in the unspoken words of the story. It was written by Elizabeth von Arnim, born Mary Annette Beauchamp and known during her lifetime simply as 'Elizabeth', after the character in her first, anonymously published novel *Elizabeth and Her German Garden*. Her first husband was Count Henning August von Arnim-Schlagenthin and she lived with him in Germany, but was herself Australian. Today, she is perhaps best known for the charming and poignant *The Enchanted April*, but readers of the Women Writers series have also recently been reintroduced to her witty, thoughtful novel, *Father*.

✻ ✻ ✻

Now that Christmas Day is done and dusted, what about other winter activities for the festive season? The first is skiing, in 'Freedom' by Nancy Morrison. It has not been possible to corroborate who the author is, because two women were writing under that name in the period. 'Freedom' appeared in *New Magazine* in 1928 – like Olive Wadsley's 'Snow' – and combines a vivid description of winter sport with a cleverer plot than first appears.

If skiing doesn't appeal, American humorist Cornelia Otis Skinner (1899–1979) can introduce us to an alternative in 'On Skating', from her collection *Excuse it, Please!* (1936). Skinner – best remembered for the irreverent travelogue *Our Hearts Were Young and Gay*, co-written with Emily Kimbrough – specialised in self-deprecating sketches, purportedly autobiographical. In 'On Skating', she gives an education in how not to approach the sport:

> Now I was ahead of my partner, now behind him; the next second found me wrapped about him like a drunkard about a lamp-post. [...] At moments we were arm's length apart, only to come together in a passionate embrace that made me feel he ought to ask me to marry him.

No festive season in Britain is complete without a trip to post-Christmas theatre – and that's where Beryl Bainbridge (1932–2010) takes us in 'Clap Hands, Here Comes Charlie', published in *Mum and Mr Armitage* in 1985. Mrs Henderson is given tickets to *Peter Pan* as a Christmas gift by a woman she cleans for, who thinks giving money would be degrading. Mrs Henderson doesn't agree, but the trip turns out to be more eventful than any of the family imagined. Bainbridge often wrote about working-class families in her eighteen novels and numerous short stories, but also turned her attention to unusual perspectives on historical events such as the sinking of RMS *Titanic* and Scott's expedition to Antarctica.

As Alec Henderson points out to his mother, *Peter Pan* isn't exactly a pantomime – "'at least not what his mother understood by the word'" – but you can experience a traditional one in Stella Margetson's (1912–1992) 'Pantomime', published in *Flood Tide and Other Stories* (1943). While the standard characters are present, we're also taken behind the scenes where we see that the line between performance and reality is more fragile for some than it should be. Margetson also wrote non-fiction about the history of pantomime, particularly in the Victorian era.

Finally, we come to a New Year's resolution in Alice Childress's (1916–1994) short piece 'On Leavin' Notes' from *Like One of the Family* (1956), composed as a series of monologues addressed by the spirited 'day worker' Mildred to her friend Marge. Childress was a novelist, short-story writer, playwright and actress, and used all those roles to question the expectations and limitations imposed on African American women in mid-century America. The title of the collection is undoubtedly ironic, and in 'On Leavin' Notes' Mildred is well aware of how she differs from the family.

And to come full circle from the turkey gutter in Alice Munro's opening story, Mildred is offered 'hanging around' turkey leftovers and rejects 'turkey hash […] turkey soup or creamed turkey'. Christmas is truly over.

Simon Thomas

Series consultant **Simon Thomas** created the middlebrow blog Stuck in a Book in 2007. He is also the co-host of the popular podcast Tea or Books? Simon has a PhD from Oxford University in Interwar Literature.

Publisher's Note

These stories, like the original novels reprinted in the British Library Women Writers series, were written and published, for the most part, in the mid-twentieth century. There are many elements of these stories which continue to entertain modern readers, however, in some cases there are also uses of language, instances of stereotyping and some attitudes expressed by narrators or characters which may not be endorsed by the publishing standards of today, and we acknowledge may continue to make uncomfortable reading for some of our audience. With this series, British Library Publishing aims to offer a new readership a chance to read some of the rare books of the British Library's collections in an affordable paperback format, to enjoy their merits and to look back into the world of the twentieth century as portrayed by their writers. It is not possible to separate these stories from the history of their writing and as such the stories are presented as originally published, with a minor edit only to the opening story. We welcome feedback from our readers, which can be sent to the following address: British Library Publishing, The British Library, 96 Euston Road, London, NWI 2DB.

The Turkey Season

ALICE MUNRO

❄

When I was fourteen I got a job at the Turkey Barn for the Christmas season. I was still too young to get a job working in a store or as a part-time waitress; I was also too nervous.

I was a turkey gutter. The other people who worked at the Turkey Barn were Lily and Marjorie and Gladys, who were also gutters; Irene and Henry, who were pluckers; Herb Abbott, the foreman, who superintended the whole operation and filled in wherever he was needed. Morgan Elliott was the owner and boss. He and his son, Morgy, did the killing.

Morgy I knew from school. I thought him stupid and despicable and was uneasy about having to consider him in a new and possibly superior guise, as the boss's son. But his father treated him so roughly, yelling and swearing at him, that he seemed no more than the lowest of the workers. The other person related to the boss was Gladys. She was his sister, and in her case there did seem to be some privilege of position. She worked slowly and went home if she was not feeling well, and was not friendly to Lily and Marjorie, although she was, a little, to me. She had come back to live with Morgan and his family after working for many years in Toronto,

– 1 –

in a bank. This was not the sort of job she was used to. Lily and Marjorie, talking about her when she wasn't there, said she had had a nervous breakdown. They said Morgan made her work in the Turkey Barn to pay for her keep. They also said, with no worry about the contradiction, that she had taken the job because she was after a man, and that the man was Herb Abbott.

All I could see when I closed my eyes, the first few nights after working there, was turkeys. I saw them hanging upside down, plucked and stiffened, pale and cold, with the heads and necks limp, the eyes and nostrils clotted with dark blood; the remaining bits of feathers—those dark and bloody too—seemed to form a crown. I saw them not with aversion but with a sense of endless work to be done.

Herb Abbott showed me what to do. You put the turkey down on the table and cut its head off with a cleaver. Then you took the loose skin around the neck and stripped it back to reveal the crop, nestled in the cleft between the gullet and the windpipe.

"Feel the gravel," said Herb encouragingly. He made me close my fingers around the crop. Then he showed me how to work my hand down behind it to cut it out, and the gullet and windpipe as well. He used shears to cut the vertebrae.

"Scrunch, scrunch," he said soothingly. "Now, put your hand in."

I did. It was deathly cold in there, in the turkey's dark insides.

"Watch out for bone splinters."

Working cautiously in the dark, I had to pull the connecting tissues loose.

"Ups-a-daisy." Herb turned the bird over and flexed each leg. "Knees up, Mother Brown. Now." He took a heavy knife and placed it directly on the knee knuckle joints and cut off the shank.

"Have a look at the worms."

Pearly-white strings, pulled out of the shank, were creeping about on their own.

"That's just the tendons shrinking. Now comes the nice part!"

He slit the bird at its bottom end, letting out a rotten smell.

"Are you educated?"

I did not know what to say.

"What's that smell?"

"Hydrogen sulfide."

"Educated," said Herb, sighing. "All right. Work your fingers around and get the guts loose. Easy. Easy. Keep your fingers together. Keep the palm inwards. Feel the ribs with the back of your hand. Feel the guts fit into your palm. Feel that? Keep going. Break the strings—as many as you can. Keep going. Feel a hard lump? That's the gizzard. Feel a soft lump? That's the heart. Okay? Okay. Get your fingers around the gizzard. Easy. Start pulling this way. That's right. That's right. Start to pull her out."

It was not easy at all. I wasn't even sure what I had was the gizzard. My hand was full of cold pulp.

"Pull," he said, and I brought out a glistening, liverish mass.

"Got it. There's the lights. You know what they are? Lungs. There's the heart. There's the gizzard. There's the gall. Now, you don't ever want to break that gall inside or it will taste the entire turkey." Tactfully, he scraped out what I had missed, including the testicles, which were like a pair of white grapes.

"Nice pair of earrings," Herb said.

Herb Abbott was a tall, firm, plump man. His hair was dark and thin, combed straight back from a widow's peak, and his eyes seemed to be slightly slanted, so that he looked like pictures of the

Devil, except that he was smooth-faced and benign. Whatever he did around the Turkey Barn—gutting, as he was now, or loading the truck, or hanging the carcasses—was done with efficient, economical movements, quickly and buoyantly. "Notice about Herb—he always walks like he had a boat moving underneath him," Marjorie said, and it was true. Herb worked on the lake boats, during the season, as a cook. Then he worked for Morgan until after Christmas. The rest of the time he helped around the poolroom, making hamburgers, sweeping up, stopping fights before they got started. That was where he lived: he had a room above the poolroom on the main street.

In all the operations at the Turkey Barn it seemed to be Herb who had the efficiency and honor of the business continually on his mind; it was he who kept everything under control. Seeing him in the yard talking to Morgan, who was a thick, short man, red in the face, an unpredictable bully, you would be sure that it was Herb who was the boss and Morgan the hired help. But it was not so.

If I had not had Herb to show me, I don't think I could have learned turkey gutting at all. I was clumsy with my hands and had been shamed for it so often that the least show of impatience on the part of the person instructing me could have brought on a dithering paralysis. I could not stand to be watched by anybody but Herb. Particularly, I couldn't stand to be watched by Lily and Marjorie, two middle-aged sisters, who were very fast and thorough and competitive gutters. They sang at their work and talked abusively and intimately to the turkey carcasses.

"Don't you nick me, you old bugger!"

"Aren't you the old crap factory!"

I had never heard women talk like that.

Gladys was not a fast gutter, though she must have been thorough; Herb would have talked to her otherwise. She never sang and certainly she never swore. I thought her rather old, though she was not as old as Lily and Marjorie; she must have been over thirty. She seemed offended by everything that went on and had the air of keeping plenty of bitter judgments to herself. I never tried to talk to her, but she spoke to me one day in the cold little washroom off the gutting shed. She was putting pancake makeup on her face. The color of the makeup was so distinct from the color of her skin that it was as if she were slapping orange paint over a whitewashed, bumpy wall.

She asked me if my hair was naturally curly.

I said yes.

"You don't have to get a permanent?"

"No."

"You're lucky. I have to do mine up every night. The chemicals in my system won't allow me to get a permanent."

There are different ways women have of talking about their looks. Some women make it clear that what they do to keep themselves up is for the sake of sex, for men. Others, like Gladys, make the job out to be a kind of housekeeping, whose very difficulties they pride themselves on. Gladys was genteel. I could see her in the bank, in a navy-blue dress with the kind of detachable white collar you can wash at night. She would be grumpy and correct.

Another time, she spoke to me about her periods, which were profuse and painful. She wanted to know about mine. There was an uneasy, prudish, agitated expression on her face. I was saved by Irene, who was using the toilet and called out, "Do like me, and you'll be rid of all your problems for a while." Irene was only a few years older than I was, but she was recently—tardily—married, and heavily pregnant.

Gladys ignored her, running cold water on her hands. The hands of all of us were red and sore-looking from the work. "I can't use that soap. If I use it, I break out in a rash," Gladys said. "If I bring my own soap in here, I can't afford to have other people using it, because I pay a lot for it—it's a special anti-allergy soap."

I think the idea that Lily and Marjorie promoted—that Gladys was after Herb Abbott—sprang from their belief that single people ought to be teased and embarrassed whenever possible, and from their interest in Herb, which led to the feeling that somebody ought to be after him. They wondered about him. What they wondered was, How can a man want so little? No wife, no family, no house. The details of his daily life, the small preferences, were of interest. Where had he been brought up? (Here and there and all over.) How far had he gone in school? (Far enough.) Where was his girlfriend? (Never tell.) Did he drink coffee or tea if he got the choice? (Coffee.)

When they talked about Gladys's being after him they must have really wanted to talk about sex—what he wanted and what he got. They must have felt a voluptuous curiosity about him, as I did. He aroused this feeling by being circumspect and not making the jokes some men did, and at the same time by not being squeamish or gentlemanly. Some men, showing me the testicles from the turkey, would have acted as if the very existence of testicles were somehow a bad joke on me, something a girl could be taunted about; another sort of man would have been embarrassed and would have thought he had to protect me from embarrassment. A man who didn't seem to feel one way or the other was an oddity—as much to older women, probably, as to me. But what was so welcome to me may have been disturbing to them. They wanted to jolt him. They even wanted Gladys to jolt him, if she could.

There wasn't any idea then—at least in Logan, Ontario, in the late forties—about homosexuality's going beyond very narrow confines. Women, certainly, believed in its rarity and in definite boundaries. There were homosexuals in town, and we knew who they were: an elegant, light-voiced, wavy-haired paperhanger who called himself an interior decorator; the minister's widow's fat, spoiled only son, who went so far as to enter baking contests and had crocheted a tablecloth; a hypochondriacal church organist and music teacher who kept the choir and his pupils in line with screaming tantrums. Once the label was fixed, there was a good deal of tolerance for these people, and their talents for decorating, for crocheting, and for music were appreciated—especially by women. "The poor fellow," they said. "He doesn't do any harm." They really seemed to believe—the women did—that it was the penchant for baking or music that was the determining factor, and that it was this activity that made the man what he was—not any other detours he might take, or wish to take. A desire to play the violin would be taken as more a deviation from manliness than would a wish to shun women. Indeed, the idea was that any manly man would wish to shun women but most of them were caught off guard, and for good.

I don't want to go into the question of whether Herb was homosexual or not, because the definition is of no use to me. I think that probably he was, but maybe he was not. (Even considering what happened later, I think that.) He is not a puzzle so arbitrarily solved.

❄

The other plucker, who worked with Irene, was Henry Streets, a neighbor of ours. There was nothing remarkable about him except that he was eighty-six years old and still, as he said of himself, a devil for work. He had whisky in his thermos, and drank it from time to time through the day. It was Henry who said to me, in our kitchen, "You ought to get yourself a job at the Turkey Barn. They need another gutter." Then my father said at once, "Not her, Henry. She's got ten thumbs," and Henry said he was just joking—it was dirty work. But I was already determined to try it—I had great need to be successful in a job like that. I was almost in the condition of a grown-up person who is ashamed of never having learned to read, so much did I feel my ineptness at manual work. Work, to everybody I knew, meant doing things I was no good at doing, and work was what people prided themselves on and measured each other by. (It goes without saying that the things I was good at, like schoolwork, were suspect or held in plain contempt.) So it was a surprise and then a triumph for me not to get fired, and to be able to turn out clean turkeys at a rate that was not disgraceful. I don't know if I really understood how much Herb Abbott was responsible for this, but he would sometimes say, "Good girl," or pat my waist and say, "You're getting to be a good gutter—you'll go a long ways in the world," and when I felt his quick, kind touch through the heavy sweater and bloody smock I wore, I felt my face glow and I wanted to lean back against him as he stood behind me. I wanted to rest my head against his wide, fleshy shoulder. When I went to sleep at night, lying on my side, I would run my cheek against the pillow and think of that as Herb's shoulder.

I was interested in how he talked to Gladys, how he looked at her or noticed her. This interest was not jealousy. I think I wanted something to happen with them. I quivered in curious expectation, as Lily and Marjorie did. We all wanted to see the flicker of sexuality in him, hear it in his voice, not because we thought it would make him seem more like other men but because we knew that with him it would be entirely different. He was kinder and more patient than most women, and as stern and remote, in some ways, as any man. We wanted to see how he could be moved.

If Gladys wanted this too, she didn't give any signs of it. It is impossible for me to tell with women like her whether they are as thick and deadly as they seem, not wanting anything much but opportunities for irritation and contempt, or if they are all choked up with gloomy fires and useless passions.

Marjorie and Lily talked about marriage. They did not have much good to say about it, in spite of their feeling that it was a state nobody should be allowed to stay out of. Marjorie said that shortly after her marriage she had gone into the woodshed with the intention of swallowing Paris green.

"I'd have done it," she said. "But the man came along in the grocery truck and I had to go out and buy the groceries. This was when we lived on the farm."

Her husband was cruel to her in those days, but later he suffered an accident—he rolled the tractor and was so badly hurt he would be an invalid all his life. They moved to town, and Marjorie was the boss now.

"He starts to sulk the other night and say he don't want his supper. Well, I just picked up his wrist and held it. He was scared I was going to twist his arm. He could see I'd do it. So I say, 'You *what!*' And he says, 'I'll eat it.'"

They talked about their father. He was a man of the old school.

He had a noose in the woodshed (not the Paris green woodshed—this would be an earlier one, on another farm), and when they got on his nerves he used to line them up and threaten to hang them. Lily, who was the younger, would shake till she fell down. This same father had arranged to marry Marjorie off to a crony of his when she was just sixteen. That was the husband who had driven her to the Paris green. Their father did it because he wanted to be sure she wouldn't get into trouble.

"Hot blood," Lily said.

I was horrified, and asked, "Why didn't you run away?"

"His word was law," Marjorie said.

They said that was what was the matter with kids nowadays—it was the kids that ruled the roost. A father's word should be law. They brought up their own kids strictly, and none had turned out bad yet. When Marjorie's son wet the bed she threatened to cut off his dingy with the butcher knife. That cured him.

They said ninety percent of the young girls nowadays drank, and swore, and took it lying down. They did not have daughters, but if they did and caught them at anything like that they would beat them raw. Irene, they said, used to go to the hockey games with her ski pants slit and nothing under them, for convenience in the snowdrifts afterward. Terrible.

I wanted to point out some contradictions. Marjorie and Lily themselves drank and swore, and what was so wonderful about the strong will of a father who would insure you a lifetime of unhappiness? (What I did not see was that Marjorie and Lily were not unhappy altogether—could not be, because of their sense of consequence, their pride and style.) I could be enraged then at the lack of logic in most adults' talk—the way they held to their pronouncements no matter what evidence might be presented to them. How could these women's hands be so gifted, so delicate and clever—for I knew they would be as good at dozens of other jobs as they were at gutting; they would be good at quilting and darning and painting and papering and kneading dough and setting out seedlings—and their thinking so slapdash, clumsy, infuriating?

Lily said she never let her husband come near her if he had been drinking. Marjorie said since the time she nearly died with a hemorrhage she never let her husband come near her, period. Lily said quickly that it was only when he'd been drinking that he tried anything. I could see that it was a matter of pride not to let your husband come near you, but I couldn't quite believe that "come near" meant "have sex". The idea of Marjorie and Lily being sought out for such purposes seemed grotesque. They had bad teeth, their stomachs sagged, their faces were dull and spotty. I decided to take "come near" literally.

❄

The two weeks before Christmas was a frantic time at the Turkey Barn. I began to go in for an hour before school as well as after school and on weekends. In the morning, when I walked to work, the streetlights would still be on and the morning stars shining. There was the Turkey Barn, on the edge of a white field, with a row of big pine trees behind it, and always, no matter how cold and still it was, these trees were lifting their branches and sighing and straining. It seems unlikely that on my way to the Turkey Barn, for an hour of gutting turkeys, I should have experienced such a sense of promise and at the same time of perfect, impenetrable mystery in the universe, but I did. Herb had something to do with that, and so did the cold snap—the series of hard, clear mornings. The truth is, such feelings weren't hard to come by then. I would get them but not know how they were to be connected with anything in real life.

One morning at the Turkey Barn there was a new gutter. This was a boy eighteen or nineteen years old, a stranger named Brian. It seemed he was a relative, or perhaps just a friend, of Herb Abbott's. He was staying with Herb. He had worked on a lake boat last summer. He said he had got sick of it, though, and quit.

What he said was "Yeah, fuckin' boats, I got sick of that."

Language at the Turkey Barn was coarse and free, but this was one word never heard there. And Brian's use of it seemed not careless but flaunting, mixing insult and provocation. Perhaps it was his general style that made it so. He had amazing good looks: taffy hair, bright blue eyes, ruddy skin, well-shaped body—the sort of good looks nobody disagrees about for a moment. But a single, relentless notion had got such a hold on him that he could not keep from turning all his assets into parody. His mouth was wet-looking and slightly open most of the time, his eyes were half shut, his expression a hopeful leer, his movements indolent, exaggerated, inviting. Perhaps if he had been put on a stage with a microphone and a guitar and let grunt and howl and wriggle and excite, he would have seemed a true celebrant. Lacking a stage, he was unconvincing. After a while he seemed just like somebody with a bad case of hiccups—his insistent sexuality was that monotonous and meaningless.

If he had toned down a bit, Marjorie and Lily would probably have enjoyed him. They could have kept up a game of telling him to shut his filthy mouth and keep his hands to himself. As it was, they said they were sick of him, and meant it. Once, Marjorie took up her gutting knife. "Keep your distance," she said. "I mean from me and my sister and that kid."

She did not tell him to keep his distance from Gladys, because Gladys wasn't there at the time and Marjorie would probably not have felt like protecting her anyway. But it was Gladys Brian particularly liked to bother. She would throw down her knife and go into the washroom and stay there ten minutes and come out with a stony face. She didn't say she was sick anymore and go home, the way she used to. Marjorie said Morgan was mad at Gladys for sponging and she couldn't get away with it any longer.

Gladys said to me, "I can't stand that kind of thing. I can't stand people mentioning that kind of thing and that kind of—gestures. It makes me sick to my stomach."

I believed her. She was terribly white. But why, in that case, did she not complain to Morgan? Perhaps relations between them were too uneasy, perhaps she could not bring herself to repeat or describe such things. Why did none of us complain—if not to Morgan, at least to Herb? I never thought of it. Brian seemed just something to put up with, like the freezing cold in the gutting shed and the smell of blood and waste. When Marjorie and Lily did threaten to complain, it was about Brian's laziness.

He was not a good gutter. He said his hands were too big. So Herb took him off gutting, told him he was to sweep and clean up, make packages of giblets, and help load the truck. This meant that he did not have to be in any one place or doing any one job at a given time, so much of the time he did nothing. He would start sweeping up, leave that and mop the tables, leave that and have a cigarette, lounge against the table bothering us until Herb called him to help load. Herb was very busy now and spent a lot of time making deliveries, so it was possible he did not know the extent of Brian's idleness.

"I don't know why Herb don't fire you," Marjorie said. "I guess the answer is he don't want you hanging around sponging on him, with no place to go."

"I know where to go," said Brian.

"Keep your sloppy mouth shut," said Marjorie. "I pity Herb. Getting saddled."

❄

On the last school day before Christmas we got out early in the afternoon. I went home and changed my clothes and came in to work at about three o'clock. Nobody was working. Everybody was in the gutting shed, where Morgan Elliott was swinging a cleaver over the gutting table and yelling. I couldn't make out what the yelling was about, and thought someone must have made a terrible mistake in his work; perhaps it had been me. Then I saw Brian on the other side of the table, looking very sulky and mean, and standing well back. The sexual leer was not altogether gone from his face, but it was flattened out and mixed with a look of impotent bad temper and some fear. That's it, I thought, Brian is getting fired for being so sloppy and lazy. Even when I made out Morgan saying "pervert" and "filthy" and "maniac", I still thought that was what was happening. Marjorie and Lily, and even brassy Irene, were standing around with downcast, rather pious looks, such as children get when somebody is suffering a terrible bawling out at school. Only old Henry seemed able to keep a cautious grin on his face. Gladys was not to be seen. Herb was standing closer to Morgan than anybody else. He was not interfering but was keeping an eye on the cleaver. Morgy was blubbering, though he didn't seem to be in any immediate danger.

Morgan was yelling at Brian to get out. "And out of this town—I mean it—and don't you wait till tomorrow if you still want your arse in one piece! Out!" he shouted, and the cleaver swung dramatically towards the door. Brian started in that direction but, whether he meant to or not, he made a swaggering, taunting motion of the buttocks. This made Morgan break into a roar and run after him, swinging the cleaver in a stagy way. Brian ran, and Morgan ran after him, and Irene screamed and grabbed her stomach. Morgan was too heavy to run any distance and probably could not have thrown the cleaver very far, either. Herb watched from the doorway. Soon Morgan came back and flung the cleaver down on the table.

"All back to work! No more gawking around here! You don't get paid for gawking! What are you getting under way at?" he said, with a hard look at Irene.

"Nothing," Irene said meekly.

"If you're getting under way get out of here."

"I'm not."

"All right, then!"

We got to work. Herb took off his blood-smeared smock and put on his jacket and went off, probably to see that Brian got ready to go on the suppertime bus. He did not say a word. Morgan and his son went out to the yard, and Irene and Henry went back to the adjoining shed, where they did the plucking, working knee-deep in the feathers Brian was supposed to keep swept up.

"Where's Gladys?" I said softly.

"Recuperating," said Marjorie. She too spoke in a quieter voice than usual, and *recuperating* was not the sort of word she and Lily normally used. It was a word to be used about Gladys, with a mocking intent.

They didn't want to talk about what had happened, because they were afraid Morgan might come in and catch them at it and fire them. Good workers as they were, they were afraid of that. Besides, they hadn't seen anything. They must have been annoyed that they hadn't. All I ever found out was that Brian had either done something or shown something to Gladys as she came out of the washroom and she had started screaming and having hysterics.

Now she'll likely be laid up with another nervous breakdown, they said. And he'll be on his way out of town. And good riddance, they said, to both of them.

❄

I have a picture of the Turkey Barn crew taken on Christmas Eve. It was taken with a flash camera that was someone's Christmas extravagance. I think it was Irene's. But Herb Abbott must have been the one who took the picture. He was the one who could be trusted to know or to learn immediately how to manage anything new, and flash cameras were fairly new at the time. The picture was taken about ten o'clock on Christmas Eve, after Herb and Morgy had come back from making the last delivery and we had washed off the gutting table and swept and mopped the cement floor. We had taken off our bloody smocks and heavy sweaters and gone into the little room called the lunchroom, where there was a table and a heater. We still wore our working clothes: overalls and shirts. The men wore caps and the women kerchiefs, tied in the wartime style. I am stout and cheerful and comradely in the picture, transformed into someone I don't ever remember being or pretending to be. I look years older than fourteen. Irene is the only one who has taken off her kerchief, freeing her long red hair. She peers out from it with a meek, sluttish, inviting look, which would match her reputation but is not like any look of hers I remember. Yes, it must have been her camera; she is posing for it, with that look, more deliberately than anyone else is. Marjorie and Lily are smiling, true to form, but their smiles are sour and reckless. With their hair hidden, and such figures as they have bundled up, they look like a couple of tough and jovial but testy workmen. Their kerchiefs look misplaced; caps would be better. Henry is in high spirits, glad to be part of the work force, grinning and looking twenty years younger than his age. Then Morgy, with his hangdog look, not trusting the occasion's bounty, and Morgan very flushed and bosslike and satisfied. He has just given each of us our bonus turkey. Each of these turkeys has a leg or a wing missing, or a malformation of some kind, so none of them are salable at the full price. But Morgan has been at pains to tell us that you often get the best meat off the gimpy ones, and he has shown us that he's taking one home himself.

We are all holding mugs or large, thick china cups, which contain not the usual tea but rye whisky. Morgan and Henry have been drinking since suppertime. Marjorie and Lily say they only want a little, and only take it at all because it's Christmas Eve and they are dead on their feet. Irene says she's dead on her feet as well but that doesn't mean she only wants a little. Herb has poured quite generously not just for her but for Lily and Marjorie too, and they do not object. He has measured mine and Morgy's out at the same time, very stingily, and poured in Coca-Cola. This is the first drink I have ever had, and as a result I will believe for years that rye-and-Coca-Cola is a standard sort of drink and will always ask for it, until I notice that few other people drink it and that it makes me sick. I didn't get sick that Christmas Eve, though; Herb had not given me enough. Except for an odd taste, and my own feeling of consequence, it was like drinking Coca-Cola.

I don't need Herb in the picture to remember what he looked like. That is, if he looked like himself, as he did all the time at the Turkey Barn and the few times I saw him on the street—as he did all the times in my life when I saw him except one.

The time he looked somewhat unlike himself was when Morgan was cursing out Brian and, later, when Brian had run off down the road. What was this different look? I've tried to remember, because I studied it hard at the time. It wasn't much different. His face looked softer and heavier then, and if you had to describe the expression on it you would have to say it was an expression of shame. But what would he be ashamed of? Ashamed of Brian, for the way he had behaved? Surely that would be late in the day; when had Brian ever behaved otherwise? Ashamed of Morgan, for carrying on so ferociously and theatrically? Or of himself, because he was famous for nipping fights and displays of this sort in the bud and hadn't been able to do it here? Would he be ashamed that he hadn't stood up for Brian? Would he have expected himself to do that, to stand up for Brian?

All this was what I wondered at the time. Later, when I knew more, at least about sex, I decided that Brian was Herb's lover, and that Gladys really was trying to get attention from Herb, and that that was why Brian had humiliated her—with or without Herb's connivance and consent. Isn't it true that people like Herb—dignified, secretive, honorable people—will often choose somebody like Brian, will waste their helpless love on some vicious, silly person who is not even evil, or a monster, but just some importunate nuisance? I decided that Herb, with all his gentleness and carefulness, was avenging himself on us all—not just on Gladys but on us all—with Brian, and that what he was feeling when I studied his face must have been a savage and gleeful scorn. But embarrassment as well—embarrassment for Brian and for himself and for Gladys, and to some degree for all of us. Shame for all of us—that is what I thought then.

Later still, I backed off from this explanation. I got to a stage of backing off from the things I couldn't really know. It's enough for me now just to think of Herb's face with that peculiar, stricken look; to think of Brian monkeying in the shade of Herb's dignity; to think of my own mystified concentration on Herb, my need to catch him out, if I could ever get the chance, and then move in and stay close to him. How attractive, how delectable, the prospect of intimacy is, with the very person who will never grant it. I can still feel the pull of a man like that, of his promising and refusing. I would still like to know things. Never mind facts. Never mind theories, either.

When I finished my drink I wanted to say something to Herb. I stood beside him and waited for a moment when he was not listening to or talking with anyone else and when the increasingly rowdy conversation of the others would cover what I had to say.

"I'm sorry your friend had to go away."

"That's all right."

Herb spoke kindly and with amusement, and so shut me off from any further right to look at or speak about his life. He knew what I was up to. He must have known it before, with lots of women. He knew how to deal with it.

Lily had a little more whisky in her mug and told how she and her best girlfriend (dead now, of liver trouble) had dressed up as men one time and gone into the men's side of the beer parlor, the side where it said MEN ONLY, because they wanted to see what it was like. They sat in a corner drinking beer and keeping their eyes and ears open, and nobody looked twice or thought a thing about them, but soon a problem arose.

"Where were we going to go? If we went around to the other side and anybody seen us going into the ladies', they would scream bloody murder. And if we went into the men's somebody'd be sure to notice we didn't do it the right way. Meanwhile the beer was going through us like a bugger!"

"What you don't do when you're young!" Marjorie said.

Several people gave me and Morgy advice. They told us to enjoy ourselves while we could. They told us to stay out of trouble. They said they had all been young once. Herb said we were a good crew and had done a good job but he didn't want to get in bad with any of the women's husbands by keeping them there too late. Marjorie and Lily expressed indifference to their husbands, but Irene announced that she loved hers and that it was not true that he had been dragged back from Detroit to marry her, no matter what people said. Henry said it was a good life if you didn't weaken. Morgan said he wished us all the most sincere Merry Christmas.

When we came out of the Turkey Barn it was snowing. Lily said it was like a Christmas card, and so it was, with the snow whirling around the streetlights in town and around the colored lights people had put up outside their doorways. Morgan was giving Henry and Irene a ride home in the truck, acknowledging age and pregnancy and Christmas. Morgy took a shortcut through the field, and Herb walked off by himself, head down and hands in his pockets, rolling slightly, as if he were on the deck of a lake boat. Marjorie and Lily linked arms with me as if we were old comrades.

"Let's sing," Lily said. "What'll we sing?"

"'We Three Kings'?" said Marjorie. "'We Three Turkey Gutters'?"

"'I'm Dreaming of a White Christmas'."

"Why dream? You got it!"

So we sang.

This Year It Will Be Different

MAEVE BINCHEY

❄

Ethel wondered had it anything to do with her name. Apart from Ethel Merman there didn't seem to be many racy Ethels; she didn't know any Ethels who took charge of their own lives.

At school there had been two other Ethels. One was a nun in the Third World, which was a choice, of course, but not a racy choice. The other was a grey sort of person, she had been grey as a teenager and she was even greyer in her forties. She worked as a minder to a Selfish Personality. She described the work as Girl Friday; it was, in fact, Dogsbody, which scanned perfectly, and after all, words mean what you want them to mean.

These were no role models, Ethel told herself. But anyway, even if it weren't a question of having a meek name, a woman couldn't change overnight. Only in movies did a happily married mother of three suddenly call a family conference and say that this year she was tired of the whole thing, weary of coming home after work and cleaning the house and buying the Christmas decorations and putting them up, buying the Christmas cards, writing them and posting them so that they would keep the few friends they had.

Only in a film would Ethel say that she had had it up to here with Christmas countdowns, and timing the brandy butter, and the chestnut stuffing, and the bacon rolls, and bracing herself for the cry "No sausages?" when a groaning platter of turkey and trimmings was hauled in from the kitchen.

She who had once loved cooking, who had delighted in her family's looking up at her hopefully waiting to be fed, now loathed the thought of what the rest of the world seemed to regard as the whole meaning of Christmas.

But there would be no big scene. What was the point of ruining everyone else's Christmas by a lecture on how selfish they all were? Ethel had a very strong sense of justice. If her husband never did a hand's turn in the kitchen, then some of the blame was surely Ethel's. From the very beginning she should have expected that he would share the meal preparation with her, assumed it, stood smiling, waiting for him to help. But twenty-five years ago women didn't do that. Young women whooshed their young husbands back to the fire and the evening newspaper. They were all mini-Superwomen then. It wasn't fair to move the goalposts in middle age.

Any more than it was fair to stage a protest against her two sons and daughter. From the start those children had been told that the first priority was their studies. Their mother had always cleared away the meal after supper to leave them space and time to do their homework, or their university essays, or their computer practice. When other women had got a dishwasher, Ethel had said the family should have a word processor. Why should she complain now?

And everyone envied her having two strong, handsome sons around the house, living with her from choice. Other people's twenty-three- and twenty-two-year-olds were mad keen to leave home. Other women with a nineteen-year-old daughter said they were demented with pleas about living in a bed-sitter, a commune, a squat. Ethel was considered lucky, and she agreed with this. She was the first to say she had got more than her fair share of good fortune.

Until this year. This year she felt she was put-upon. If she saw one more picture of a forty-seven-year-old woman smiling at her out of a magazine with the body of an eighteen-year-old, gleaming skin, fifty-six white, even teeth, and shiny hair, Ethel was going to go after her with a carving knife.

This year, for the first time, she did not look forward to Christmas. This year she had made the calculation: the thought, the work, the worry, the bone-aching tiredness on one side of the scales; the pleasure of the family on the other. They didn't even begin to balance. With a heavy heart she realised that it wasn't worth it.

She didn't do anything dramatic. She didn't do anything at all. She bought no tree, she mended no fairy lights, she sent six cards to people who really needed cards. There was no excited talking about weights of turkey and length of time cooking the ham as in other years. There were no lists, no excursions for late-night shopping. She came home after work, made the supper, cleared it away, washed up and sat down and looked at the television.

Eventually they noticed.

"When are you getting the tree, Ethel?" her husband asked her good-naturedly.

"The tree?" She looked at him blankly, as if it were a strange Scandinavian custom that hadn't hit Ireland.

He frowned. "Sean will get the tree this year," he said, looking thunderously at his elder son.

"Are the mince pies done yet?" Brian asked her.

She smiled at him dreamily.

"Done?" she asked.

"Made, like, cooked. You know, in tins, like always." He was confused.

"I'm sure the shops are full of them, all right," she said.

Ethel's husband shook his head warningly at Brian, the younger son.

The subject was dropped.

Next day Theresa said to the others that there was no turkey in the freezer, nor had one been ordered. And Ethel turned up the television so that she wouldn't hear the family conference that she knew was going on in the kitchen.

They came to her very formally. They reminded her of a trade-union delegation walking up the steps to arbitration. Or like people delivering a letter of protest at an embassy.

"This year it's going to be different, Ethel." Her husband's voice was gruff at the awkward, unfamiliar words. "We realise that we haven't been doing our fair share. No, don't deny it, we have all discussed it and this year you'll find that it will be different."

"We'll do all the washing-up after Christmas dinner," Sean said. "And clear away all the wrapping paper," added Brian. "And I'll ice the cake when you've made it. I mean after the almond icing," Theresa said.

She looked at them all, one by one, with a pleasant smile, as she always had.

"That would be very nice," she said. She spoke somehow remotely. She knew they wanted more. They wanted her to leap up there and then and put on a pinny, crying that now she knew they would each do one chore, then she would work like a demon to catch up. Buzz, buzz, fuss, fuss. But she didn't have the energy, she wished they would stop talking about it.

Her husband patted her hand.

"Not just words, you know, Ethel. We have very concrete plans and it will begin before Christmas. Actually it will begin tomorrow. So don't come into the kitchen for a bit, we want to finalise our discussions."

They all trooped back to the kitchen again. She lay back in her chair. She hadn't wanted to punish them, to withhold affection, to sulk her way into getting a bit more help. It was no carefully planned victory, no cunning ploy.

She could hear them murmuring and planning; she could hear their voices getting excited and them shushing each other. They were trying so hard to make up for the years of not noticing. Yes, that is all it was. Simply not noticing how hard she worked.

It just hadn't dawned on them how unequal was the situation where five adults left this house in the morning to go out to work and one adult kept the house running as well.

Of course, she could always give up her job and be a full-time wife and mother. But that seemed a foolish thing to do now, at this stage, when the next stage would be the empty nest that people talked about. They were all saving for deposits, so they didn't really give her much, and they were her own children. You couldn't ask them for real board and lodging, could you?

No, no, it was her own fault that they hadn't seen how hard she worked and how tired she was. Or hadn't seen until now. She listened happily to the conversation in the kitchen. Well, now they knew, God bless them. Perhaps it hadn't been a bad thing at all to be a bit listless, even though it hadn't come from within, it wasn't an act she had put on.

Next morning they asked her what time she'd be home from work.

"Well, like every day, around half-past six," she said.

"Could you make it half-past seven?" they asked.

She could indeed, she could have a nice drink with her friend Maire from work. Maire, who said that she was like a mat for that family to walk on. It would be deeply satisfying to tell Maire that she couldn't go home since the family were doing all the pre-Christmas preparations for her.

"You could always go to the supermarket," Theresa said.

"Am I to do any shopping?" Ethel was flustered. She had thought they were seeing to all that.

She saw the boys frown at Theresa.

"Or do whatever you like, I mean," Theresa said.

"You won't forget foil, will you?" Ethel said anxiously. If they were going to do all this baking, it would be awful if they ran out of things.

"Foil?" They looked at her blankly.

"Maybe I'll come back early and give you a bit of a hand ..."

There was a chorus of disagreement.

Nobody wanted that. No, no, she was to stay out. It was four days before Christmas, this would be a Christmas like no other, wait and see, but she couldn't be at home.

They all went off to work or college.

She noticed that the new regime hadn't involved clearing away their breakfast things, but Ethel told herself it would be curmudgeonly to complain about clearing away five cups and saucers and plates and cornflake bowls and washing them and drying them. She wanted to leave the kitchen perfect for them and all they were going to do.

She wondered that they hadn't taken out the cookery books. She would leave them in a conspicuous place, together with all those cookery articles she had cut from the paper and clipped together with a big clothes-peg. But she must stop fussing, she'd be late for work.

Maire was delighted with the invitation to a drink after work. "What happened? Did they all fly off to the Bahamas without you or something?" she asked.

Ethel laughed; that was just Maire's way, making little of the married state.

She hugged her secret to herself. Her family who were going to do everything. Things were exciting at the office, they were all going to get new office furniture in the new year, the old stuff was being sold off at ridiculous prices. Ethel wondered would Sean like the computer table, or would Brian like the small desk. Nothing would be too good for them this year. But then, did second-hand goods look shabby, as if you didn't care?

With the unaccustomed buzz of two hot whiskeys to light her home, Ethel came up the path and let herself in the door.

"I'm back," she called. "May I come into the kitchen?"

They were standing there, sheepish and eager. Her heart was full for them. While she had been out drinking whiskey with lemon and cloves in it, stretching her legs and talking about the new office layout with Maire, they had been slaving. Poor Maire had to go back to her empty flat, while lucky Ethel had this family who had promised her that things would be different this year. She felt a prickling around her nose and eyes and hoped that she wasn't going to cry.

She never remembered them giving her a treat or a surprise. This is what made this one all the better. For her birthday it had been a couple of notes folded over, from her husband, a request to buy herself something nice. Cards from the children. Not every year. And for Christmas they clubbed together to get her something that the house needed. Last year it had been an electric can opener. The year before it had been lagging for the cylinder.

How could she have known that they would change?

They looked at her, all of them waiting for her reaction. They wanted her to love it, whatever they had done.

She hoped they had found the candied peel—it was in one of those cartons without much identification on it, but even if they hadn't she'd say nothing.

She looked around the kitchen. There was no sign of anything baked or blended or stirred or mixed or prepared.

And still they looked at her, eager and full of anticipation.

She followed their eyes. A large and awkward-looking television set took up the only shelf of work space that had any length or breadth in it.

An indoor aerial rose from it perilously, meaning that the shelves behind it couldn't be got at.

They stood back so that she could view the full splendour of it.

Sean turned it on with a flourish, like a ringmaster at a circus. "Da-daaaaa!" he cried.

"I *told* you this Christmas was going to be different to the others." Ethel's husband beamed at her.

From now on she could look at television as well as the rest of them; she'd be as informed and catch up on things and not be left out, just because she had to be in the kitchen.

All around her they stood, a circle of goodwill waiting to share in her delight. From very far away she heard their voices. Sean had known a fellow who did up televisions, Dad had given the money, Brian had gone to collect it in someone's van. Theresa had bought the plug and put it on herself.

Years of hiding her disappointment stood to Ethel at this moment. The muscles of her face sprang into action. The mouth into an ooooh of delight, the eyes into surprise and excitement; the hands even clasped themselves automatically.

With the practised steps of a dancer she made the movements that they expected. Her hand went out like an automaton to stroke the hideous, misshapen television that took up most of her kitchen.

As they went back to wait for her to make the supper, happy that they had bought her the gift that would change everything, Ethel got to work in the kitchen.

She had taken off her coat and put on her pinny. She edged around the large television set and mentally rearranged every shelf and bit of storage that she had.

She felt curiously apart from everything, and in her head she kept hearing their voices saying that this Christmas was going to be different.

They were right, it felt different; but surely it couldn't be on account of this crass gift, a sign that they wanted her forever chained to the kitchen cooking for them and cleaning up after them.

As she pricked the sausages and peeled the potatoes it became clear to her. They had done something for her for the very first time—not something she wanted, but something; and why?

Because she had sulked. Ethel hadn't intended to sulk but that's exactly what it had been. What other women had been doing for years. Women who had pouted and complained, and demanded to be appreciated. By refusing to begin the preparations for Christmas, she had drawn a response from them.

Now, what more could be done?

She turned on the crackling, snowy television and looked at it with interest. It was the beginning. She would have to go slowly, of course. A lifetime of being a drudge could not be turned around instantly. If, as a worm, she was seen to turn too much, it might be thought to be her nerves, her time of life, a case for a nice chat with some kind, white-coated person prescribing tranquillisers. No instant withdrawal of services. It would be done very slowly.

She looked at them all settled inside around the flat-screen television, satisfied that the Right Thing had been done, and that supper would be ready soon. They had no idea just how different things were indeed going to be from now on.

General Impressions of a Christmas Shopping Centre

E.M. Delafield

Christmas comes but once a year ... General Impression, waxing stronger every hour, that even this is rather overdoing it.

In Our Oriental Bazaar, which displays a profusion of brass ash-trays, raffia bags, hand-painted almanacs, and an occasional carved blackwood elephant to add local colour, about eighty-five ladies, one gentleman, and a sprinkling of children, are competing for the services of Two Young Ladies.

A SHOPPER. What about Uncle *Ernest*? He doesn't *smoke*, and he doesn't *drink*.

HER FRIEND (understanding that this handsome testimonial merely denotes the limitations imposed upon choosing a present for Uncle Ernest). That makes it so *difficult*, I always think. What about a fire-screen? For when he sits over the fire in the evenings, I mean.

THE SHOPPER (doubtfully). Well—he might like it. But I think he always goes to his Club in the evenings, and he wouldn't want to carry it *about* with him. ... The orange china frog is rather quaint, isn't it?

THE FRIEND. Sweet. But I like the hand-screen *better*, I think. I mean, I think it is more *useful*.

THE SHOPPER (severely). Still, dear, it isn't what *you* like, is it? It's what Uncle *Ernest* would like.

She realizes too late that this pungent snub has, in some mysterious way, the effect of committing her to the Orange Frog, for which she subsequently pays, with great reluctance, the sum of seven shillings and sixpence. General Impression that if she expects any enthusiasm about it from Uncle Ernest, she is being unduly optimistic.

A SOLITARY GENTLEMAN (timidly). I'll take these Christmas cards, please.

A SALES-LADY. Sign, please.

Sign, in the person of a Gentleman in a Frock coat, materializes, bowing affably from the waist.

THE SALES-LADY. Six at six-three, two at nine and a half, one Pock-Cal. at one-eleven-three, and six at a penny-three. Sign, please.

General Impression that Sign hasn't the faintest idea what she means, but will willingly execute a perfectly illegible flourish with a pencil on the bill, in order to get the whole business over and done with.

❄

In the Toy Department, the floor being entirely packed with shopping Mothers, Aunts, Grand-mothers, nurses, governesses, and children, a Christmas Novelty is displayed in the shape of a dejected-looking Santa Claus, driving a Real Sleigh drawn by eight Real Ponies.

PRACTICALLY EVERY MOTHR IN THE PLACE. Oh, look, darling. Why, there's *Santa Claus!*

General Impression that half the infants present are in tears, between fatigue, bewilderment, and alarm at the appearance of the ponies, and that the other half are only to be held back by brute force from wrecking the whole equipage in their excitement.

❄

In the Groceries.

A POLITE VOICE. And what can I have the pleasure of doing for you, madam?

A VAGUE LADY. I really want a *Biscuit,* that I used to know very well years ago, but that one simply never *sees,* nowadays.

A pause, as though either the owner of the Polite Voice or the Lady herself might here break into a short poem—*Amitié d'Autrefois*, or something like that, after the style of François Villon, suggested by the subject. Instead of which:

THE V. L. Not a *Cheese* biscuit, and yet not exactly a *Sweet* biscuit. Something between the two, if you know what I mean.

THE P. V. (with more suavity than sincerity). Perfectly, madam.

THE V. L. (confidentially). We used to like them so much as *children*, you know, and I've always wanted to get a tin of them for my *own* children. I'm afraid I can't remember what they were called, but the *shape* was oval—rather a *small* oval.

The P. V. continues to assent to these, and similar, pieces of information with unabated brightness and readiness. General Impression that between them they will probably run the lost gems to earth in the end, but that it will all take *Time*.

❄

On the Ground Floor, the Jewellery Department, unlike any other, exhibits more salesmen than customers. A Moleskin Wrap is, however, talking to a Nutria Coat in the centre aisle.

THE M.W. My dear, they're really rather twee—long ruby drops, you know, set in platinum—Peter's Christmas present.

THE N. C. My dear—he *doesn't* wear earrings, does he?

THE M.W. My dear, what an idea! His Christmas present to *me*, of course. He does so hate shopping in all the crowd that I always do it *for* him, you know.

THE N. C. My dear, how sweet of you! I wonder if Paul would like *me* to do that—?

General Impression that whether he would or not, this is what will happen.

✳

MOST PEOPLE (sooner or later). Well, what one always feels is that Christmas is the *children's* festival. ...

Exeunt, to engage usual table for the usual dinner-dance at the usual London restaurant.

The Christmas Pageant

Barbara Robinson

The Herdmans were absolutely the worst children in the history of the world. They lied and stole and smoked cigarettes (even the girls) and used bad language and hit children smaller than themselves, and cussed their teachers and took the name of the Lord in vain and set fire to Fred Shoemaker's old fallen-down pigsty. Everybody was delighted about this last, because the pigsty was an eyesore. People said it was the only good thing the Herdmans ever did and added that, had the Herdmans *known* it was a good thing, they wouldn't have done it. They would have set fire to something—or somebody—else.

They were so all-round awful that they were almost mysterious: six skinny, stringy-haired, sharp-featured children as much alike as a string of cut-out paper dolls in assorted sizes. They moved from class to class through Woodrow School like death watch beetles, nibbling away at the fortitude and good intentions of one teacher after another, and they seemed headed straight for the bad end so widely predicted for them—until they ran foul of the church and my mother.

Mother wasn't out to store up gold stars in heaven or even to improve conditions here on earth for the likes of Herdmans. She just happened to get stuck with the Christmas pageant when Mrs. Armstrong fell and broke her leg.

There was never anything very novel or outstanding about our Sunday school Christmas pageant—beyond a certain annual astonishment that it got put on at all—and Mother did not plan any innovations. The script, of course, was standard, as were the costumes, and there were few surprises in casting: the babies' class were angels; intermediate children were shepherds; big boys were Wise Men; Alan Hopkins, the vicar's son, was Joseph; my friend Alice Wendle was Mary, because she was so bright, so neat and clean and, above all, so pious. The rest of us made up the angel choir, lined up according to height, because nobody could sing parts anyway. Now and then an unexpected talent would blossom. Somebody would produce a trombone and play a halting accompaniment to *The First Noël,* or an elocution student would recite *What Child is This?* One year a girl whistled two of the five carols, for something different—but people felt that was just a little *too* different.

Mostly, though, it was just the Christmas story, performed year after year in lacklustre fashion by a troupe of jaded actors in bath towels and sheets.

No-one ever thought about the Herdmans in connection with the Christmas pageant. Each year in September, Mr. Hopkins invited them to join Sunday school, as he did all the children in the neighbourhood who were not otherwise affiliated; but they never came—and for those of us who spent the week in school being pounded and poked and pushed about by Herdmans, Sunday was truly a day of rest. Once we had to write on a piece of paper what we liked best about Sunday school, and my little brother, Bobby, wrote: "No Herdmans." His Sunday school teacher said that wasn't a very Christian sentiment; but Mother said it was a very practical one, since Bobby had spent the whole of one term black-and-blue because he had to sit next to Stanley Herdman at school.

It was probably Bobby's fault that the Herdmans appeared at Sunday school that year. He told Stanley that we got refreshments, which was a lie. We got little chocolate eggs at Easter and lemonade and biscuits on Children's Day, but Bobby made it sound like a feast every Sunday, and the Herdmans came, expecting chocolate cake and ice cream. They stayed, I suppose, out of curiosity and returned spasmodically through the autumn, still looking for refreshments—or so we thought. It never occurred to anyone that they were looking for anything else. Perhaps it never occurred to them.

Then, with Christmas hard upon us, it was time to get ready for the pageant. Announcements were made in Sunday school, and Imogene Herdman dug me in the ribs with her elbow and demanded, "What's a pageant?"

"It's a play," I said, and Imogene looked interested. All the Herdmans were avid filmgoers. One or two of them would create a disturbance at the front of the cinema while the others slipped in. Like professional criminals, they had the good sense to split up once they got inside, so the manager could never locate all of them and throw them out before the picture was over.

"What's the play about?" Imogene asked.

"It's about Jesus," I told her.

"Everything here is," she said.

Mrs. Armstrong, who was advising Mother from her sick bed, said it was very important to give all the children an opportunity to volunteer for the major rôles, but she said it was merely a matter of form. So Mother went before the assembled Sunday school, with paper and pencil, quite unprepared for what was to befall her.

She left, half an hour later, in a state of shock at the prospect of a Christmas pageant in which the Holy Family and the Wise Men would be portrayed by Herdmans—Ralph, Imogene, Stanley, Claude and Ollie. There was one Herdman left over—Gladys, who was younger and, if possible, nastier than all the rest—and Mother, in her confusion at this unexpected turn of events, cast Gladys as the Angel of the Lord who brings the good news to the shepherds. Two or three more timid shepherds promptly resigned on the grounds that Gladys was small but mighty and any good news she brought would be accompanied by a thump on the head.

Mother told those shepherds not to be so silly (though her voice lacked conviction), and she asked Alice Wendle why in the world she hadn't raised her hand to be Mary.

"I don't know," Alice said bleakly, but I knew. I had heard Imogene telling Alice what would happen to her if she raised so much as one finger to volunteer for anything.

"You know she wouldn't do all those things she said," I told Alice as we walked home.

"Yes, she would," Alice said. "Herdmans will do anything. But your mother should have told her no. Somebody should put her out of the pageant—all of them."

Alice was not alone in this opinion. Her mother, for instance, made a speech about it to all her friends and said it was little short of sacrilege to let Imogene Herdman portray Mary. Others agreed, but based their objection on the more practical grounds that the church could ill afford whatever damage the Herdmans might do. Mr. Hopkins took the only stand he could in his position and reminded the outraged ladies that when Jesus said, "Suffer the little children to come unto me," He meant all the little children, including Herdmans.

The first rehearsal for the pageant was always the worst, with twenty or thirty children milling round the church hall, fussing and fighting, some of the younger ones crying from sheer excitement, and most of the older ones sullen and resigned but bored to death by the whole thing. This year, however, was different. There was a feeling of anticipation in the air—everyone was waiting to see what the Herdmans would do.

They arrived ten minutes late, sidling into the hall for all the world like a bunch of Chicago gangsters about to stage a massacre. Mother had saved six seats at the front, where she could keep all of them under her eye, and they took these seats with reasonable grace. Stanley, as he passed Bobby, knuckled him behind the ear, and one of the tinies yelled out suddenly as Gladys went by. But I had heard Mother say that she was going to ignore everything except blood, and since the tiny wasn't bleeding and neither was Bobby, nothing happened.

Mother started to separate everyone into angels, shepherds and guests at the inn, but she at once ran into a basic hitch. The Herdmans turned out to know practically nothing about the Christmas story. They knew that Christmas was Jesus's birthday, but all other details were news to them: the shepherds, the Wise Men, the star, the stable, the crowded inn.

"'There was in the days of Herod, the king,'" Mother began, and we all settled ourselves on the Sunday school chairs, looking bored. "'... Mary his espoused wife, being great with child ...'"

"Pregnant!" yelled Ralph Herdman.

We were all shocked, and there was a low swell of embarrassed giggles, which Mother stopped by hammering on the floor with a blackboard pointer. "That's enough, Ralph," she said, and went on with the story.

"I don't think it's very nice to say Mary was pregnant," Alice Wendle whispered to me.

"But she was," I pointed out. In a way, though, I agreed with Alice—it seemed like too commonplace a condition and too coarse a word for Mary. "Great with child" sounded better.

"I'm not even supposed to know what pregnant means." Alice folded her hands in her lap and pinched her lips together. "I'd better tell my mother."

"Tell her what?"

"That your mother is talking about things like that in church. My mother might not want me to be here."

❄

I was pretty sure Alice would do it. She wanted to be Mary, and she was furious with Mother. I knew, too, that she would make it sound worse than it was and that Mrs. Wendle would get even more annoyed than she already was. But there wasn't much I could do about it, except pinch Alice, which I did. She yelped, and Mother separated us and made me sit beside Imogene Herdman and sent Alice to sit in the middle of the baby angels.

I wasn't keen to sit next to Imogene, but she didn't even notice me—not much, anyway. "Shut up," was all she said to me. "I want to hear her."

I was astonished. Among other things, the Herdmans were famous for never sitting still and never paying attention to anyone—teachers, parents (their own or anybody else's), the welfare worker, the police—yet here they were, eyes glued on my mother and taking in every word.

"What's that?" they would yell from time to time when some word or phrase escaped their comprehension, and when Mother read about there being no room at the inn, Imogene's jaw dropped and she cried out, "My God! Not even for Jesus?"

I saw Alice purse her lips, so I know that that was something else Mrs. Wendle would hear about—swearing in the church.

The Herdmans couldn't seem to get past the part about no room at the inn, although Mother explained that after all nobody knew the baby was going to turn out to be Jesus. Nevertheless, Imogene continued to mutter, "Her pregnant and everything."

A lot of time was spent on the Wise Men, because of the myrrh and the frankincense; but the Herdmans finally dismissed all three as cheap skates for bringing such rotten presents. Stanley made a brief, profane observation about the Wise Men, and that *did* make Mother jump, but she pretended not to hear and pressed on.

Of course, when they heard about Herod, they recognised the real villain. "Who's going to be Herod in this play?" Stanley asked.

"We don't show Herod in our pageant," Mother told him, and he was obviously disappointed.

I couldn't understand the Herdmans' attitude. They had involved themselves totally in the events of the first Christmas, much as my mother's friends involved themselves with the people and events in television serials. Similarly, the Herdmans hoped for a bloody end to Herod, worried about Mary ("pregnant and everything") and longed to set fire to the inn.

To me, the story was too familiar to arouse such passions, and too firmly entrenched in the whole fabric of Sunday school lessons for me to see it as a separate drama. And it never once occurred to me that, for perhaps the first time in their lives, the Herdmans were on the right side of some issue.

It occurred to Mother, though, and surprised her. She said it seemed to show a faint hint of Christian conscience. My father didn't agree. "As far as I can see, you base your optimism on the fact that they wanted to see Herod buried alive. Pretty thin ice."

"I know, but aren't you surprised it's Herod they want to see done in and not the baby?"

Father stared at her for a minute. "What *did* happen to Herod?"

Mother looked blank. "I don't know." She turned to me and asked, "Do you know?"

I had never thought about Herod—he was just a name, a person in the Bible, lacking any reality: Herod-the-king.

But the Herdmans looked him up somewhere and reported, with considerable disgust, that he had died in bed of old age. It almost turned them against the pageant—it seemed too tame an end for the chief villain.

Anybody, like Alice, who had hoped that the Herdmans would get bored with the whole thing and walk out, was doomed to disappointment. They came to every rehearsal, on time, and learned their lines and behaved—for them—with remarkable self-control. Of course, three or four new boxes of crayons disappeared from the Sunday school cupboard, and both cloakrooms were always blue with smoke after rehearsals; but I did notice that Imogene, before lighting up, was careful to remove her Mary costume, which indicated a nice sense of the fitness of things.

Most of all, they added a new dimension to what was for the rest of us pretty familiar stuff. Lacking any sort of religious exposure, they seemed to feel none of the reverence usually associated with these proceedings. Imogene, for instance, didn't know that Mary was traditionally portrayed with downcast eyes and distant manner. In Imogene's hands, Mary became triumphant, fiercely protective and a little bossy. "Get away from the baby!" she yelled at Ralph, who was Joseph, and she made the Wise Men keep their distance.

"The Wise Men want to honour the Christ Child," Mother explained. "They don't intend to harm Him, for goodness' sake."

But the Wise Men were something new and different, too, and no-one could blame Imogene for being wary of them. You got the feeling that *these* Wise Men were going to hustle back to Herod as fast as they could and squeal on the baby. Such faulty interpretations made things difficult for Mother, but they made the rehearsals electric with excitement for everybody eke.

Of course, with childish faith, we all knew that the story would turn out all right in the end, but for the first time we sensed an element of possibility and doubt.

"What if we *didn't* go home some different way?" Stanley demanded, in his rôle of Melchior. "What if we went back and told on the baby?" What if, indeed? we all thought, suddenly struck by this revolutionary notion.

"He would murder Jesus," Ralph stated. "The king —what's-his-name."

"He would not!" Imogene yelled, fire in her eye, and since the Herdmans fought one another just as readily as they fought everybody else, Mother had to step in and smooth these curiously troubled waters.

I thought about it later, though, and decided that if Herod, a king, set out to murder Jesus, the baby son of a carpenter, he would surely find some way to do it. And the answer to Stanley's question was so staggering in its implications that I put it right out of my mind.

And just as Herod-the-king had now acquired personality—I pictured him looking something like Rasputin—I also had a new slant on Jesus. Influenced by pictures, by the unfamiliar language of the Bible, by the unexplainable mysteries of Jesus's life, I had always thought of Him as a somewhat mystical person dressed in a long white nightgown and surrounded always—as He walked on water or through air—by a kind of electrical nimbus that protected Him and immobilised others. This was not, to be sure, what I had been taught, but it was what I had figured out—until Stanley Herdman posed his hypothetical question and made me aware of Jesus as a baby, who had to be dressed and undressed, fed and cared for, just like anybody else.

❄️

Whether others were similarly enlightened, I didn't know. Alice Wendle, for one, was not. "I don't think it's very nice to talk about the baby Jesus being murdered," she said, stitching her lips together and looking sour. That was one more thing to tell her mother, if and when she decided to. Mrs. Wendle was a member of four church ladies' organisations and could rally a lot of support if she wanted to. But whether she could sabotage the pageant was questionable, so Alice was waiting for the Herdmans to do something so outright pagan that it could not be ignored.

"Be sure and tell your mother that I can step in and be Mary if I have to," she told me as we stood in the back row of the angel choir, "and if I'm Mary, I can get Mrs. Perkins's baby for Jesus. But Mrs. Perkins won't let Imogene Herdman get her hands on him." Alice looked quite smug about this, because she knew that the baby—or lack of one—was a sore point with my mother.

In the beginning, there was a wide variety of candidates for that rôle, all the way from the youngest Sloper, who was not quite three weeks old, up to Billy Cooper, who was almost four but could, his mother said, "scrunch up." But when all these mothers learned about the Herdmans, they withdrew their babies.

Imogene offered to steal one, but Mother said no, we would use my old baby doll—which, surprisingly, pleased Imogene. "A doll can't bite you," she pointed out, which seemed to indicate that Herdmans started out vicious from the cradle.

As we drove to the church hall on Christmas Eve, my father asked what he should expect, and Mother smiled. "Something different," she said.

It didn't seem any different, though, at first. There was the usual confusion and clatter; baby angels got poked in the eye by other baby angels' wings; grumpy shepherds stumbled round in voluminous bath towels; the spotlight swooped wildly up and down and to and fro before focusing on the manger scene; part of the angel choir got stuck behind the piano; and *Away in a Manger* was pitched, as usual, much too high.

But when Mary and Joseph took their places—stiff as statues, selfconscious to the point of paralysis—I felt a funny little shiver up my spine, even in the close quarters of the angel choir. Though Ralph and Imogene knew exactly what they were to do and where to sit or stand, they seemed uncertain now—like refugees sent to wait in some strange place, with all their belongings around them.

That's how it must have been for the Holy Family, I thought— stuck away in a stable by people who didn't really much care what happened to them. They must have been a little tattered too, like this Mary and Joseph (Imogene's veil was cockeyed and Ralph's hair stuck out all round his ears).

Imogene had my baby doll, not cradled in her arms but slung up over her shoulder, and before she put it in the manger she thumped it twice on the back—habit, maybe, or instinct.

I heard Alice Wendle gasp, and she poked me in the ribs. "Isn't she awful!"

"No," I said. "She's scared."

"Of what?" Alice whispered. "Herdmans aren't scared of anything or anybody on earth." Then her eyes widened, and her mouth popped open, and she stared at me. "Do you think they're scared of God?"

"I think they've just found out about Him," I said

For Alice and me and all the rest of us, accustomed to the mysteries of the Christmas story, there was for the first time reality to it, too: a baby, a troubled mother, an anxious father and, arriving from the East (like my uncle from Suffolk), some rich friends. But for the Herdmans, accustomed only to what they could see and hear and touch (or steal or smoke or set fire to), there was, apparently for the first time, a sense of the universal wonder that Christmas brings.

It made the pageant different—no doubt about that—and when it was over, people stood round the lobby of the hall arguing about why it was different. There was something special, everyone agreed, though they couldn't put their finger on just what.

Mrs. Wendle said, well, Mary the mother of Jesus had a black eye: that was something special. But only what you might expect.

Actually, it wasn't what you might expect. Nobody hit Imogene and she didn't hit anybody else. She just walked into the corner of the Sunday school cupboard, in a kind of daze. All the Herdmans were in a kind of daze throughout the performance, as if they had only just realised what it was all about. Only Gladys was herself: "Hey! Unto you a child is born!" she hollered, as if it was indeed the best news in the world. But Mary and Joseph and the Wise Men seemed as struck by awe as, probably, the first ones were.

❄

After the pageant, there were toffees and small gifts for everyone, but Imogene asked Mother for a set of the Bible-story pictures, instead. "Can you imagine that?" Mother said later. "She took out the picture of Mary and said it was exactly right—whatever that means."

I suppose it *was* exactly right for Imogene—the pretty, unreal, softly draped figures in the Bible pictures. But for most of the rest of us, forever after, Mary was Imogene Herdman, with her straggly hair escaping from underneath a cheesecloth veil, clutching my doll like grim death and daring anyone up to and including King Herod to lay a finger on her baby.

The Wise Men were always Stanley Herdman and his

brothers—Greeks bearing gifts, who had a change of heart or were scared to death of Mary, and so went home a different way.

And the Angel of the Lord was no golden-haired young girl with harp and wings, but Gladys Herdman, with her skinny legs and battered sandals sticking out under her robe, her halo lopsided and her face beet-red with excitement, bellowing at the shepherds, as if they were not only terrified, but deaf: "Hey! Unto you a child is born!"

Ticket for a Carol Concert

AUDREY BURTON

❄

Mrs. Lorimer thought it would be easy to sell tickets for the carol concert in the village hall. Most people, she believed, liked singing carols, and on the Saturday before Christmas everybody would be feeling Christmassy and quite willing to part with sixpence to help buy toys for the local Children's Home. The choir had been practising for weeks and had now amassed a goodly repertoire of carols old and new. The audience would enjoy singing the well-known carols.

The thick bundle of tickets Mrs. Lorimer had set out with had dwindled to a thin dozen. She had just a few more calls to make, and soon all her tickets ought to be gone.

❄

Mrs. Jenks wiped one hand on the corner of her apron and thought "Good gracious, what mother of three young children had time to spend gallivanting about on the Saturday before Christmas at a carol concert? Even if Harry would stay in and mind the children there was too much to be done at home. She had nothing against carols, mind you. She liked them when the singers came round the street. You could listen to the singing while you rolled out the pastry for the mince-pies. "It's the kids, you see," she told Mrs. Lorimer. "I couldn't leave the kids, but I'll buy a ticket as it's for the children. Children's toys, you said, didn't you?"

❄

Mr. Sage lived alone and was something of a philosopher. Some people called him a highbrow, and Mr. Sage could always be depended on to go an independent way of his own and pour ridicule on established customs. "My dear Mrs. Lorimer," he said patiently—"Christmas carols in the year 1950! But just look at the world! Look at it! Look at Korea! Look much nearer home. And you ask me to sing 'Peace on earth and mercy mild.' Haven't you heard of the atom bomb? 'Once in Royal David's City,' you'll sing. What's happened to Royal David's City, I ask you? You ask me to come along and sing a nice few carols. Bah! Nothing but hypocrisy!" He'd give a donation towards the children's toys, but why couldn't she ask for it in a straightforward manner instead of all this humbug about singing carols?

❄

Miss Sweeting was a singer, a professional singer. She got engagements sometimes with the B.B.C. and at Masonic dinners. "A carol concert!" She gave a delicate, artistic shudder. No, she really couldn't listen to amateurs, couldn't hear all that music being murdered by people who hadn't been trained how to produce their voices properly. "I'm sorry," she told Mrs. Lorimer, "but there is a music programme on the wireless I particularly want to hear that night." Oh, it was for the children, was it? She would, of course, be pleased to buy a ticket, but Mrs. Lorimer mustn't expect to see her at the concert.

❄

Mrs. Wright-Wrightson-Wright was new to the village. Her husband had recently bought the old-fashioned Gables and spent nearly a fortune modernising it. When Mrs. Lorimer called, Mrs. Wright-Wrightson-Wright was counting cocktail glasses and wondering whether to order another dozen. "A carol concert! How quaint!" she rippled. "But the Saturday before Christmas! No. I'm having a cocktail party that evening … just a few friends," she added. Some of her town friends were coming, and she was going to invite a selected few of the local people who mattered. "I've got a few friends coming in for a drink." She was going to say: "I wonder if you would to join us?"

"Why not bring along your friends?" suggested Mrs. Lorimer. "It would give the party a real Christmas flavour."

Mrs. Wright-Wrightson-Wright couldn't suppress a giggle. Her friends from town would not appreciate the opportunity of hearing a few earnest rustics singing away. How too prehistoric, they would say. But she'd better buy a ticket, thought Mrs. Wright-Wrightson-Wright. Village people expected you to support their affairs, and if it would help along her popularity in a new place she would have six tickets. It would be cheap at the price.

✸

Mr. Verity put down his pen and wondered how he was ever going to finish writing his new book if he couldn't be free of interruptions. He was a scientist doing a really worthwhile bit of research, and to help out the meagre income accorded to scientists who do this work, he was writing a popular book on "*Cosmic Rays.*" Usually he left his wife to make his polite excuses for this kind of thing, but his wife was away. A carol concert, indeed! Things that you couldn't see under a microscope or prove mathematically left him cold. Show him Christmas under a microscope and he would be interested.

No, he was afraid he was much too busy writing his new book to go to a carol concert, he excused himself. Now why didn't the woman go away? She still stood there twiddling a ticket about in her hand. Oh, it was for the local Children's Home, was it? Now he understood, his hand went to his pocket. If he gave the woman two shillings she'd clear off and he could get on with his writing. He stuffed the ticket in his pocket.

✸

On Saturday night Mrs. Jenks was feeling tired. She had put the children to bed and her husband Harry was reading the paper. She had just finished icing the cake and had now perched a jolly Father Christmas on top. The children would like that. The cake looked a treat with the white icing all ruffed up to look like real snow. She took the mince-pies out of the oven and thought that was another job done. Now she would sit down and ask Harry for a piece of the paper he wasn't reading. Or ought she to darn the socks? She reached for her spectacles on the mantelshelf and her eyes fell on the ticket for the carol concert. "Remember how you and I used to sing in the choir?" she asked her husband.

"Aye, I do. Like to go to-night?" he asked his wife. "I could pop across the road and ask mother to come in and mind the kids. Be like old times, wouldn't it? You go and put your hat on while I pop along and fetch mother. Do you good to leave that mending."

❄

Mr. Sage had just finished Chapter 1 of his book. It made pretty gloomy reading. Here we were, making all the same mistakes we had made before and heading straight for another war. Why was it that man should strive to annihilate himself? Individuals were decent enough. All this strife and bitterness among the nations. Where could you find the answer? *"Oh, hush the noise, ye men of strife"*—the words came to him out of the blue and he couldn't place them for a minute or so. The words seemed fitted to a tune; how did it go? *"Oh, hush the noise, ye men of strife."* … Oh yes, he remembered … *"And hear the angels sing."*

No doubt they'd be singing at that carol concert to-night. A lot of well-meaning people who couldn't do a thing against the forces of aggression. Of course, if all men of strife would hush it might be different. But what could one person do, what could a whole village do? Oh well, it was a dull book. Everything he'd read so far had been said before. He might as well toddle off to the village hall. Not that it would make the slightest difference. But it would be a gesture!

Miss Sweeting put another lump of coal on the fire, got out two volumes of music scores and switched on the radio. By the comfort of her own fire she was going to have an enjoyable evening listening to music as it should be sung. The set took a little time to warm up, but instead of the pure liquid sound of musical voices, all Miss Sweeting got was a rasping blare. She twiddled the switch, but the rasping blare persisted. Something had gone wrong with the set. The same thing had happened once before and then it was a defective valve. She looked at the mahogany-coloured box with distaste. It was too bad that her radio should let her down like this just before Christmas. Miss Sweeting hadn't reckoned on an evening's silence. She looked wistfully at the music books and the music she couldn't hear. "I wonder what sort of a dreadful noise they are making in the village hall?" she wondered suddenly. Half the audience wouldn't be capable of singing in tune . . . they'd go terribly flat on the top notes and they'd get the dotted notes in the wrong place. A good strong soprano voice might help them a little, and at least it would be something to have one person in the hall singing correctly. Now where had she put that ticket?

❄

Mrs. Wright-Wrightson-Wright put her hands on the radiators and thought what a blessing central heating was. The old-fashioned house was now looking something like a smart modern house. The ultramodern decorating and the modern furniture had helped. But in spite of all these modern improvements, in spite of the lavish assortment of expensive drinks, she was alone. Her friends in London had made excuses. Someone who had just taken over a new studio was throwing a party, and they must go and see the place. The selected people in the village she had telephoned were sorry, but they were going to the carol concert. A lonely evening stretched before her, because her husband had telephoned that he had made a new business contact that might turn out pretty useful, and he wouldn't be home. The windows rattled, and suddenly she felt the loneliness was more than she could stand. She would go to the carol concert! It might be amusing.

❄

Mr. Verity paused for a moment trying to think of a simple word to explain a complicated bit of science. He was writing against time, his publishers were clamouring for his manuscript. Interest in cosmic rays was the big thing at the moment, they told him. He had been writing late night after night and he found it difficult to stay awake. Even strong black coffee wouldn't help much. He'd go for a short brisk walk and try to freshen himself up. Ten minutes he would allow himself, no more.

He stepped out into the cold night, and walked briskly. The sky was clear and starry. One day, perhaps, he thought science would wrest from the sky its secrets. Always the heavens had mystified man. Wasn't it a star in the East that the three wise men had followed? That's what they would be singing about at the carol concert to-night. Most unscientific astronomy, of course. What did those three wise men know about the stars and their set courses, he wondered. As though to find the answer, he stepped into the village hall.

✳

The village hall was crowded. When the concert started only the back row was empty, but now, Mrs. Lorimer noted happily, even that row was full. That nice little couple, Mr. and Mrs. Jenks must have found someone to look after their children, because there they were in the back row sharing a hymn-book and singing heartily. Mrs. Wright-Wrightson-Wright must have put off her cocktail party, because there she was, looking quite happy and much nicer without that superior condescending look. It was nice to see and hear Miss Sweeting, too. Her strong soprano voice was proving a great help at the back of the hall. Mrs. Lorimer must remember to thank her afterwards. Mr. Sage was there, too, and not looking at all gloomy now. His voice was booming out and he was singing as though he enjoyed it. And next to him was Mr. Verity. Mrs. Lorimer had never hoped to lure him away from his scientific works.

"*Peace on earth,*" came the voices, and everyone, even those in the back row, sang as though they meant it.

Snow

Olive Wadsley

Speeding along, keeping to a level forty-five, John's heart sang within him. Another ten miles or so, and he'd be there—and she'd be there.

He hadn't brought his man with him from purely sentimental reasons, because he felt so sentimental ...

So—"You'd like to spend Christmas with your wife, eh, Spalding?"

And Spalding's slow, gratified grin:

"Well—sir, if it wouldn't make so much difference, if you could manage—!"

This evening, John felt he could manage the world.

Almost, he was persuaded, Viola loved him ... There had been times, moments, which were unforgettable ... a dance, two weeks before, when he had felt certain, holding her close, then closer, that his heart must be beating straight into hers, so hard had it thudded, and looking down, had seen her eyes close for a second ... her lashes had lain like ebon shadows on her cheeks, and above, just below his chin, her hair had burnt bright gold.

Violetta, Vi-Vi, "V"—everyone seemed to have a special name for her amongst her own "crowd," as she called her friends.

They were outside John's life rather, those twenty-to-thirty girls and men, with their quick marriages, quicker partings, their utter reserve, which was only surpassed by their complete frankness!

A world which had never intrigued him … this "younger set," with its special code of morals, and its special lack of 'em!

John's chill Northern outlook—that of a man, moreover, who had worked—had not bred much understanding of this particular type.

He had never bothered about it, until he had met Viola.

He could recall that first meeting, as if it had been an hour ago (only five more miles to Charteris!). Last June, at Gibson's: one of those set dinners … Gibson always had an eye to business: you weren't asked if you had no "pull" … John had been patently aware his inside knowledge about the Steel Combine had been the reason for his own invitation … He also, however, had wished to know about a certain stock, so he had gone.

Viola Frayle had sat next to him, and confided to him lightly:

"I really oughtn't to be here at all, y'know! I don't fit in! My cousin Dodo Rexe was asked, and has hay fever! So I was proposed, and was accepted! So difficult, isn't it, to find someone to fill in bang in the middle of the season!"

John had made a rather ponderous, obvious reply, and then, somehow, they had begun to talk, really talk.

Very thin, he'd thought her—too thin … and too much lipstick … but it hadn't been lipstick, after all! A miracle of lovely, natural colouring, in these days! Not pretty, but beautiful hair, lashes, and that vivid mouth—but not pretty, all the same.

Something more than pretty, fascinating enough to tear the heart from your body.

Discreetly, as became his thirty-five years, his big position, his reputation for having a "heavy character," John had tried to learn something of Viola Frayle.

"Oh, rotten poor, the lot of 'em. One married Rexe, but they can't keep the place up, I hear. There are three of 'em, I believe. War hit old Frayle devilish hard."

Rotten poor, or not, devilish hard hit, or not, Viola, Vi-Vi, "V" seemed to get about very comfortably!

John knew this, for the simple reason he had taken to "getting about" too, tracking Viola down, and then appearing surprised when he met her.

Viola said to her sister Theodore, who was known as Dodo:

"Cast the eye over one John Mallington, will you? The steel magnate young man, tall, and dour, and with a chin to him, and I should say, a temper. Tragically, he's rolling, I learn!"

Lady Rexe said:

"Darling, are you serious? And if so, why tragically? Thank Heaven, he *is* rolling. Steel, d'you say? I'll ask Bill—"

Bill replied so encouragingly that his wife kissed him.

"Oh, Bill, if he only would! For I believe Vi-Vi cares!"

Viola had begun to ask herself that question rather often:

"Do I—don't I?"

In certain ways John was so maddening: he would seem to be growing a little near to her, and then, abruptly, go away again, become, in an instant, the rather aloof, very cautious man she had met first of all.

"He's certain to think it's for his money," Viola decided wearily; "he's bound to, with his temperament — and knowing our poverty!"

If she had known John had angled for an invitation to Charteris, her heart, too, would have sung within her.

But John had been so roundabout, had become possessed of such a reputation for aloofness, that kindly Miles Charteris would never have dreamt of asking him, had John not dropped (as it had seemed) into a game at the Club two weeks earlier (on the evening of the day he had learnt Viola was to spend Christmas at her cousin's!) and drifted in the next evening, and then given Miles an excellent American tip, and then, finally, discussed Christmas.

"We're having a bit of a party. Why not come down and join us?" Miles had suggested hospitably.

John had accepted that invitation, very definitely, then and there, and yesterday he had bought Viola's present: it lay against his heart now, not entirely for romantic reasons, but that inner pocket, in which it reposed, was a very safe one! "It" was a string of pearls.

John put his hand against the flat case: safe, all right!

He tried to think of fastening the pearls about Viola's white neck, and found that thought made him accelerate wildly.

Only two miles now, and he'd be there … Two minutes, and he'd be looking at Viola.

It was stingingly cold; the lights from the village windows glowed like yellow diamonds, as clearly and hard.

"Going to snow, I bet," John thought, and recalled the dull orange sky, as he had been sliding out of London.

What had Charteris said: "You pass a white gate, and then, a hundred yards on, you'll see the lodge?"

John saw it, the high iron gates stood wide open, he spun into the drive, it was a long one, with a turn just at the end.

"Hullo, what a jolly-looking house—lovely place—turrets and all, and a terrace —and all lit up, and a huge door," which as John hooted, was flung wide and let out a stream of aromatic air, of laughter, light and warmth. Then Miles Charteris, the most genial of hosts, and his wife, who was comfy and kindly. A lot of other people, too—but, really, only Viola, clad in woolly things of some dark colour, looking as slender as a boy, Viola giving him a hand which, as he touched it, thrilled him through and through, Viola saying in a cool, low voice:

"Had a good run down?"

"Rather, yes, excellent—very good," John told her confusedly, helping himself to toasted crumpet, and tea, and cake, all together.

"He *does* love me," Viola decided, and could not meet John's eyes.

He never left her: he felt wild with delight, happier than he had ever been in all his life, glad, for Viola's sake, of his riches, glad of his strength, glad it was Christmas time, eager for it to be Christmas Day.

"Got the Christmas spirit?" he asked Viola boyishly, and she said, quite eagerly for her:

"Oh, I have! But I always do have! I begin to feel excited quite early, you know, and then when it gets to Christmas Eve, I don't know, but I feel—oh, rather as if I were waiting for something wonderful to happen! And very young! The second I smell the Christmas tree, I lose every year except five. I'm five again, and I believe in Santa Claus, and that Christmas is the loveliest time in all the year, and hearing church bells ringing makes me want to cry a little, and hearing the waits in the night *does* make me cry!"

"So do I—I mean—I mean I understand," John said huskily.

He could *see* her, a baby of five, led down to the tree, gazing at it with just the same wide, grey eyes she had now.

"I simply hate people who put on frills and tell you they are bored stiff with Christmas, and it's only a time for overeating and then sleeping it off!" Viola went on, in the same warm, quick voice: "To me, it's the one time you are really a child at heart, however old you may be. It's a time of lovely, darling surprises, of, for once, reaping the benefit of having saved up—of being happy just simply … One walks lots at Christmas, have you noticed? And one plays games, and is not only a child at heart, but pure of heart; just for a little while."

John was adoring her; words seemed of no use to him at all.

"And if only it snows!" she broke out. "Pray that it does! I want snow more than anything!"

"It's going to. I'll see that it does!" John promised her.

They stayed in their firelit corner; someone had started the gramophone, others began to dance; Viola and John sat on, sometimes silent, sometimes talking.

John had never seen this Viola, who was not once "clever," or laughed too wisely.

"This is the real Viola," he told himself.

They even went together to see the children in the nursery.

"No chance of their going to sleep at all, Miss," old Nanny told Viola severely. "What with their stockings and all, and now visitors."

"Now, darling, now, now!" Viola said, and kissed her. Old Nanny smiled then:

"You go along, my lamb, back to your party."

Viola told John: "It was this Nanny who used to lead me in when I was five!"

"And a nice handful you were, too," Nanny observed complacently.

John, six-foot-two, dark, and not really very prepossessing to look upon, was vowing over Viola's bright head that some day— some day ... he'd—they'd have a nursery-some day ... and a baby to lead round a Christmas-tree.

Almost, he told Viola he loved her; out in the long gallery, he was just wondering if he could get the words out, and trying to make his throat feel less like a chalk pit when Viola cried:

"Oh, it's snowing!"

If she had had the least idea John was just going to try and tell her he loved her, nothing on earth would have made her speak at all, but seeing his last remark had been concerning the excellent central heating arrangements, she had really had no reason to know his state of mind.

And, down in the big hall again, a man came forward, a very good looking young man indeed, of thirty or so, blonde, lithe, and horribly self-assured. He had been dancing when John and Viola had walked down the wide, shallow oaken stairs, but he sped away from his partner now and up to Viola, and seized her hands, and said:

"Vi-Vi, my darling!" and kissed her.

Viola said, a tiny flame of lovely colour in either cheek:

"Paul, where on earth have you sprung from?"

"Is that your welcome home for the wanderer?" Paul demanded, he seemed to laugh, but his eyes were not amused.

"See you later," he told Viola, and sped off again.

"Paul Trent's a sort of cousin," Viola said flatly to John, who replied: "I see."

One of those silences which are so crushing, fell between them, constraint grew momentarily. Then someone asked Viola to dance, and she left John.

He watched her morosely.

Saw Paul Trent leave his partner again, wheel Viola's from her, and take her himself, and dance away with her.

They talked, John noticed, earnestly, all the time, and vanished finally.

Pulling aside the curtains when he had finished changing, John saw a white world ... it was snowing heavily now.

He flung a window wide, and just then someone else, too, did the same thing, and then wonder of wonders! Viola's face looked out. She saw John, and called "Hullo!" softly.

She was two rooms away, a terrace ran the whole length of the east wing.

"Let's greet the first snow!" Viola called, almost in a whisper.

They stepped out on to the terrace, and stood beneath the soft sky, the snow-flakes falling on them.

Viola, glancing down at their footprints, pointed her small satin shoe at the deep print of John's big foot and said:

"Bon jour, Monsieur!"

He bent above her, laughing, too, and touched the imprint of her shoe with his foot, and answered:

"Bon jour, Madame!"

He nearly told her then ... A church bell struck the hour; it was still, after that deep, clear noise, with that stillness which seems a little like a benediction, it is so kind and somehow gentle. And then, just as John was going to speak, the gong boomed out, and from a window further down still, Paul Trent stepped, called out: "Aha!" and came towards them.

They all three went in through Viola's window, and John had a second's glimpse of a silken wrap on the chintz-covered chair beside the fire, some clean, sweet scent came to him, he saw Viola's bed, so white and blue, and young somehow ... then they were all on the stairs running down together, and some of John's disappointment was assuaged because Viola's hand touched his, Viola's arm touched his, and he found he was to sit next to her at dinner.

"I'll tell her after," he swore.

But he didn't get the chance; she went off with Lady Charteris, and most of the other girls, to finish the Tree, and the men began to play poker.

Paul Trent played brilliantly; he won at first, then he struck a run of bad luck.

He finished about a hundred down, and Miles Charteris did not like it.

He told John so.

"Hate these young fellas playing so high in my house—a party like this, specially. Christmas party, I mean."

"Who is Trent?" John asked.

"Well, a kind of second cousin of my wife's—related to the Frayle's really. Thought just after the war, Vi and he'd make a match of it. But he's wild, y'know. Unstable. Brilliant fella' and all that, but, I dunno—" He laughed his jolly laugh.

"You know how it is—some fella's failings you can put the finger on straight away; Paul's you can't!"

John carried away only that sentence: "Thought Vi and he'd make a match of it—"

Christmas Eve was marvellous, for the sun shone on snow, and the air was like spiced wine, and John sat beside Viola in the car when they all went shopping, and he knew her arm *did* touch his, not by accident.

They walked together, too, all the time, only alas, others walked "fore and aft of 'em," as John communed wrathfully within himself.

And after tea, to his bitter amazement, Viola went off with Lady Charteris in the car.

Trent got up another poker game, and lost again.

"Young fool!" John thought contemptuously, not having played.

He went up to his room early to dress; at least he'd have that "before dinner" few minutes, he decided grimly, and he sent Viola a tiny note to her room, saying:

"May I greet Madame on the terrace this evening?"

Rather neat for old John, for he was not given to pretty phrasing.

He hurried desperately over his dressing, then flung wide the long window, and waited.

And Viola's voice said:

"Bon soir, Monsieur!"

John forgot even the dark whiteness of the snow; he simply went forward and took Viola in his arms, and took her mouth, and kissed and kissed it, and said at last:

"Give me your heart!"

She answered, looking up into his eyes:

"Oh, John, you had it long ago," and then she whispered:

"Feel, my darling, how it belongs to you," and pressed his hand hard on her heart. "It's trying to get to you, that's why it leaps so!"

He was lost in love for her, lost in wonder, and the shyest, yet wildest adoration.

In her room, they clung for one long minute together, mouth to mouth, then just as they turned to go, Viola drew John back. She opened the window a tiny way:

"Look—our footsteps ... you can't tell whose is which—!"

And John, his arm about her, said with a real flight of imagining, for him:

"Think when you *really* say '*Bon jour, Monsieur!*'"

Viola had never been slow in all her life, she leant her face up and drew his down, and said against his lips:

"Ah, but think when I *really* say '*Bon soir!*'"

❄

They could not give their secret to the world yet, but when Viola danced with Paul, and John saw him talking, talking again, he felt inclined to go up and seize her in his arms, and tell Paul:

"Cut it out—she's mine!"

The man had an indefinable air of possessing Viola as they danced.

"Dammim!" John thought savagely.

Viola and he stole away to say good night, and he forgot Paul, forgot everything and everyone, save Viola, that she loved him.

He went back to say good night to Miles, to find yet another game had started.

Miles said to him gloomily, staring at Paul: "Heaven knows how he can do it; he's lost a packet again."

John did not care; he scarcely thought of Paul, or even kindly, distressed Miles. He went off to bed, walking on the stars, Heaven his to clasp, because Viola had lain in his arms.

Very sentimentally, he looked for the footprints again, but the snow had coveted them up; it was falling now heavily, drifting down in flakes so big, the air seemed filled with white butterflies. A note struck softly and sonorously, another, and with a quick stirring of his heart John realised that midnight had come, that Christmas Day was beginning.

He felt he had to share his very first Christmas of all with Viola.

And he'd the pearls to give her!

Anything, anyway, for an excuse to see her again.

He drew on his coat, and went out into the corridor, and knocked on her door.

Viola answered at once:

"Yes? Who is it?"

"It's John. I say, come to the door, just for a minute!"

She came at once, looking very young indeed, in a little white silk dressing gown, which had an absurd bit of swansdown making a snowball sort of edging on the collar.

John kissed her eagerly; neither he nor she knew which of them entered the room, who thrust the door to, gently.

"Christmas Day. Our first!" John whispered against her lips.

His cheek to hers, one arm close about her, he ordered:

"Shut your eyes, darling!"

"They are shut, the better to feel your kisses, John!"

The gift of the string of pearls was put off again.

John whispered at last:

"Bend your head, just for a minute!"

Viola bent it, it needed very little action on her part, for it was resting on John's heart. He slid the gleaming softness of the pearls about her neck.

"Happy Christmas, and all my love!"

Another clock striking, struck them both with amazement.

One!

"I must go," John said.

"I think you must, darling!"

And as they kissed a "really last kiss," as Viola said, Paul Trent came on light feet down the corridor, halted before the slightly-open door, knocked, called gently:

"Vi-Vi—you there?"

John flung the door wide and Paul said, very expressively indeed:

"Hullo-o—!"

His eyes laughed at them.

John said instantly, more curtly than he knew:

"Like to offer me congratulations, Trent? I have the great honour to be going to marry Viola."

Paul was effusive, very gay indeed: he passed on, leaving them with a very unsubtle remark, for him, about "two being company, who were keeping company—!"

He had spoilt the perfection of their good night.

Viola shivered a little.

"You're cold, darling," John said instantly, and kissing her a real last kiss, left her.

He lay awake a long time, and somehow his mood of exaltation could not be recaptured; he hounded down the reason at last:

Trent's call to Viola outside her door!

The first jealousy he had ever known warred in his heart with his first happiness.

He tossed, and turned, he heard three, four strike, then he decided to get up, and let in more air.

He opened the window noiselessly, it had stopped snowing, the air blew on his face icy and somehow splendid; he loved it and stood there, his warm dressing-gown about him, drinking in frozen, exhilarating cleanliness.

Everything looked very distinct; the carved stone balustrade of the terrace seemed very high ... the snow stood thick on it.

Then he looked at Viola's window, and then he looked down.

His gaze fastened on her footprints with sickening tenacity: he could not lift his eyes. The footprints—two lines of them ... leading from her window to Trent's.

He had to be sure; he went out, bare-footed and bent down ... he knew her footprint all right!

She had gone to Paul Trent's room ... come back from it.

Laboriously, John effaced the footprints; he went back into his room.

He stared at the walls about him ... only walls, a few panes of glass kept him from her.

The blood rushed into his head in a boiling torrent, left it again, and he felt very cold. He was dazed, bewildered. That Viola could leave him and go to Trent ... He'd waited all these years to find the one woman to whom he could give everything ...

A sound, a tiny rustling sound, roused him; it came from under the door: he was across the floor in two huge, noiseless strides and had flung wide the door; his grip got someone, someone's hair, soft hair, then a shoulder; he held that in a vice as he switched on the light, and saw kneeling at his feet, Viola, and, pushed just inside his room, an envelope.

He stood over her, his hands clenching and unclenching, his eyes, sunk in his head, blazing; Viola was looking up at him, amazedly.

John's hand shot out, gripped her shoulder again, pulled her to the window. He opened it, and told her in a whisper, pointing to the smoothed snow:

"I effaced your footprints, which led to Trent's room, and away from it!"

Viola had been half clinging to him; now she drew away, and a mask seemed to settle over her face.

"Bad luck that, for you and me—that you saw them!" she said.

John glared at her.

And then she asked him, in the same level voice:

"John, do you love me?"

His lips twitched.

"You must give me an answer."

He gave her one.

"Fool that I am, I do—"

Viola's face softened then; she put out a hand, and then drew it back.

"Believing me a ... believing I have betrayed everything lovely, and decent, and fine ...?"

He nodded heavily.

"Even then."

"Oh, John!"

There was a note in her voice, a note of gladness, which seemed to get at his very heart and stab it; the rage which had shaken him and exhausted him, gathered strength again ... She thought she could get away with it, did she? ... She'd better—better —get—out.

He said so, his voice a hoarse mutter:

"Get out—*now*—"

Viola flung out a hand.

"No, you've got to hear. We've a chance of happiness, you and I, that very few people have. We're not, either of us, easy sort of natures. I mean, I fought against—against loving you ... and you—I'm not really the sort of woman you wanted to love! I wasn't, anyway. But love beat both of us —wiped out our different standpoints ... dislikes—everything. In the envelope you hold I've tried to tell you everything ... I've told you, too, all about Paul, about my seeing him to-night. It's my Christmas present to you ... the real story of my heart, the real gift of it! I—I felt I couldn't give you anything but the very best of me, and the rest, too. Paul brought a note to me to-night, when you'd left me, telling me he loved me so much he wouldn't give me up ... that, if I didn't break with you, and marry him, he'd tell you everything.

"John, it was a very foolish but rather pathetic everything ... And when I wrote the truth of it to you, I didn't do it lest Paul should tell you, but because I want to start clear with you ... as *new* as—as the shining snow we greeted together! This is all the story: Two years ago Paul and I ran away—he was married then ... I—I ran back. I found I didn't care, that I'd never cared really. Paul was decent then, when I told him. He let me go, and he kept silence. He always has, till now. No one knew. There was nothing wrong to know; but there's only my word for that ... I mean, ordinary people wouldn't accept it! I think seeing me so—so terribly in love with you, divining it, I suppose, made Paul suddenly insanely jealous. When I'd read his letter, I never stopped to think. I went to his window and knocked, and he came to the window, and we talked. He was sorry then; he tore up his letter ... he said he'd not meant it. He was decent, anyway, you see. But I knew I must tell you. I couldn't risk your being hurt through me—by me, yes, but not—not because of my cowardice. So I tried to be brave and I wrote to you … that's all."

John said in a whisper:

"My dear …"

She shook her head, tears were in her eyes now:

"Oh, *am* I your dear?"

He caught her to him. Accidentally, her foot touched his, between tears and laughter and kisses, she whispered to him:

"Bon jour, Monsieur!"

'Twas the Night
Before Christmas

By Kate Nivison

The mouse had been waiting a long time for this moment. Usually the house went quiet much earlier, and it was safe to venture out of the tiny hole behind the sideboard on the nightly hunt for crumbs. Recently, she'd been collecting nesting materials too—bits of fluff from the new carpet were her favourite, and the odd corner nibbled from a newspaper. It was a good house for mice.

Whiskers a-twitch, she peered out at the soft glow from the Christmas tree lights, and then shrank back almost at once. One of Them was still there, asleep in the big armchair. It wasn't safe even yet.

The woman in the armchair had meant to be in bed by twelve. Every year it was the same. Start earlier, she's told herself—like straight after the summer holiday, perhaps! This year she really had tried, but every Christmas things got more complicated. For a start, the children got bigger and more certain about what they definitely didn't want for Christmas.

"Honestly, Mum, can't you tell Nan nobody wears stuff like that," followed by perennial wails of "But I don't want a 'good' book!"

This year the children had gone right over the top and put in for a party—on Christmas Eve, of all days. The prospect of it flashed briefly across the woman's dreaming mind and almost woke her in a fright. In the end they'd settled for a promise of one at New Year on condition that Dad made the punch and they all went home by one o'clock—take it or leave it. They'd taken it, with sighs of "Oh, Mum". Maybe fourteen and twelve was still a bit young to be worrying about orgies, and they weren't so grown up that they didn't expect a bulging stocking a-piece as well as something big. Each Christmas Eve, they took longer to get to bed, and … The woman's head nodded gently forward as she willed everything to go quiet.

The mouse hovered a moment longer, then tried a nervous dash to the corner of the sideboard and paused to sniff at a curl of purple foil the vacuum cleaner had missed. It smelt promising, sweetish, but there was nothing left inside to eat and it wasn't soft enough for the nest. There was no more movement from the giant in the chair, but the next cover was behind the parcels under the tree. The kitchen seemed a long way off to a mouse who didn't feel like running so fast tonight, so she collected some loose fluff into a ball and left it there. Something better might turn up, and she had to find a bite to eat.

The eyelids of the woman in the chair were flickering, and her face had a faint, almost foolish smile, but there was no one to see. Part of her mind was remembering that once, when she had been about ten, she had come downstairs herself on Christmas Eve to have a peek at the presents and found her mother dozing in the chair just like this. There had been fewer presents then. They hadn't been poor exactly—at least it hadn't seemed like it at the time. Had it been easier in those days, with less choice, less expected? Mum had never made a fuss. Nothing much had seemed to change from year to year, but there had been a kind of magic ... Maybe it was instinct. Tomorrow when they all came, she would ask her if there was some secret to it that she should know about. Tomorrow. It was still worth it, though—every bit of it, and maybe one day she'd get the knack ...

Round the tree, a few fallen pine needles were sticking in the carpet. The mouse avoided them. They smelt odd and tasted worse. Last night she'd climbed to the first branch, but there were only more needles and some kind of silver straw hanging all over it. It was no good for a nest, and there wasn't a berry anywhere. But in the kitchen, there'd been a real feast—fatty crumbs of pastry, a currant or two and a half-eaten cream biscuit between the oven and the cupboard. Just thinking about it made her sit up and clean her whiskers. She always seemed to be hungry these days.

The jean-clad leg of the figure in the chair gave a little twitch. By the time she'd cleaned up after an emergency batch of mince pies, and settled down to fill the stockings, she was ready to drop, but quite content. The presents under the tree were all wrapped and labelled, and the fairy-lights were working again after blowing a fuse. The fuse mender had retired to bed with a large whisky, saying to wake him up, ho-ho, when the stockings were ready and it was quiet enough to creep in and deliver the goods. He'd said this for the last five years at least, and she never had. So she'd settled down to her last and best task on Christmas Eve—the stockings—with a mug of warm milk topped up with a dash of brandy, and a wonky home-made mince pie. It was so warm and quiet …

The mouse, frightened by the twitching leg, glanced towards the chair, where she saw something on the floor that made her almost squeak with excitement. Near the chair was a plate, and plates meant food.

Then—panic. The woman's head gave a sudden movement and the leather armchair creaked. For a second, the eyes opened, then closed again sleepily, but the mouse was already behind a large coloured box.

In a split second of consciousness, the woman's sleepy gaze fell on the old picture frame full of Christmas cards she'd pinned against the red velvet backing. From family and friends, they were all there, and what an odd assortment they were—plain and fancy, elegant and rude, classical and cheeky, meaningful and daft—and a lot of well-wishers would be round tomorrow. Tomorrow. Just the thought of it was enough to force her awake. Shaking her head, she looked round her, remembering. The stockings, of course. She was supposed to be filling them. Now, that was for Jeremy, that for Michelle …

Half way to the plate, the mouse panicked and changed direction. Yesterday some sort of strange box affair had appeared on the coffee table by the tree. It was full of little painted figures and straw—real straw. If she could just get to it and stay there until the giant went away. It wasn't too difficult because the presents were piled up round it. Carefully, so as not to disturb the paper wrappings which were slippery and made rustling noises, the mouse edged along, then missed her footing and had to cling on to some ribbon. The noise was deafening. The giant must have heard.

But, oh horrors, what was this? The Other One had suddenly put his head round the door and boomed something about parking his reindeer.

The woman jumped and so did the mouse. "Oh, you wretch! I thought you'd gone to sleep."

"Me, sleep on Christmas Eve, with you still slaving away down here? Now would I do a thing like that?"

The woman looked up at him and laughed. "Actually, I think I must have dropped off. It's funny, just as you came in I thought I heard a sort of scuffling over by the tree. You don't suppose we've got mice, do you?

"Probably some needles falling off. I still like a real tree though."

"M'mm," said the woman, not entirely convinced on either count. "Are the kids asleep yet? Honestly, this year is the last time I'm going through this performance. They can come and get their stockings down here in the morning. They're too old for this."

"Yes, but *I'm* not. You know you like it really. Come on, the coast's clear." He held out his giant arms, and the woman got up stiffly and stretched. The shadows merged and fell across the mouse's hiding place.

"Pass me up the mug and plate, love." The woman gave a yawn. "If I bend down once more today, my back will go."

"Oh, leave them down there. We'll have a good clear up in the morning." He picked up the crackling stockings and felt their weight. "You're good at this, you know," he said. "I'm glad I married someone who's good at Christmas."

"Suppose we've got mice?"

"A house like this wouldn't be complete without a moose loose aboot it. M'mm, you smell of warm milk and brandy and mince pie. Give us a kiss."

The mouse had to wait a long time for the last whisperings and creaks to die down upstairs, but it was worth it. There were some tasty crumbs, sugar and currants on the plate, and the straw in the new box was just right for the nest. A few more trips and she would be able to rest, ready for what tomorrow would bring.

And then, and only then, was it really quiet enough in the house for Christmas to come in.

Christmas Fugue

MURIEL SPARK

❄

As a growing schoolgirl Cynthia had been a nature-lover; in those days she had thought of herself in those terms. She would love to go for solitary walks beside a river, feel the rain on her face, lean over old walls, gazing into dark pools. She was dreamy, wrote nature poetry. It was part of a home-counties culture of the nineteen-seventies, and she had left all but the memories behind her when she left England to join her cousin Moira, a girl slightly older than herself, in Sydney, where Moira ran a random boutique of youthful clothes, handbags, hand-made slippers, ceramics, cushions, decorated writing paper, and many other art-like objects. Moira married a successful lawyer and moved to Adelaide. Beautiful Sydney suddenly became empty for Cynthia. She had a boyfriend. He, too, suddenly became empty. At twenty-four she wanted a new life. She had never really known the old life.

So many friends had invited her to spend Christmas day with them that she couldn't remember how many. Kind faces, smiling, "You'll be lonely without Moira. ... What are your plans for Christmas?" Georgie (her so-called boyfriend) "Look, you must come to us. We'd love you to come to us for Christmas. My kid brother and sister. ..."

Cynthia felt terribly empty. "Actually, I'm going back to England." "So soon? Before Christmas?"

She packed her things, gave away all the stuff she didn't want. She had a one-way air ticket, Sydney–London, precisely on Christmas day. She would spend Christmas day on the plane. She thought all the time of all the beauty and blossoming life-style she was leaving behind her, the sea, the beaches, the shops, the mountains, but now it was like leaning over an old wall, dreaming. England was her destination, and really her destiny. She had never had a full adult life in England. Georgie saw her off on the plane. He was going for a new life, too, to the blue hills and wonderful colours of Brisbane, where his only uncle needed him on his Queensland sheep farm. For someone else, Cynthia thought, he won't be empty. Far from it. But he is empty for me.

She would not be alone in England. Her parents, divorced, were in their early fifties. Her brother, still unmarried, was a city accountant. An aunt had died recently; Cynthia was the executor of her will. She would not be alone in England, or in any way wondering what to do.

❄

The plane was practically empty.

"Nobody flies on Christmas day," said the hostess who served the preliminary drinks. "At least, very few. The rush is always before Christmas, and then there's always a full flight after Boxing day till New Year when things begin to normalize." She was talking to a young man who had remarked on the number of empty seats. "I'm spending Christmas on the plane because I'd nowhere else to go. I thought it might be amusing."

"It will be amusing," said the pretty hostess. "We'll make it fun."

The young man looked pleased. He was a few seats in front of Cynthia. He looked around, saw Cynthia and smiled. In the course of the next hour he made it known to this small world in the air that he was a teacher returning from an exchange programme.

The plane had left Sydney at after three in the afternoon of Christmas day. There remained over nine hours to Bangkok, their refuelling stop.

Luxuriously occupying two vacant front seats of the compartment was a middle-aged couple fully intent on their reading; he, a copy of *Time* Magazine, she, a tattered paperback of Agatha Christie's: *The Mysterious Affair at Styles*.

A thin, tall man with glasses passed the couple on the way to the lavatories. On his emergence he stopped, pointed at the paperback and said, "Agatha Christie! You're reading Agatha Christie. She's a serial killer. On your dark side you yourself are a serial killer." The man beamed triumphantly and made his way to a seat behind the couple.

A steward appeared and was called by the couple, both together. "Who's that man?"—"Did you hear what he said? He said I am a serial killer."

"Excuse me sir is there something wrong?" the steward demanded of the man with glasses.

"Just making an observation," the man replied.

The steward disappeared into the front of the plane, and reappeared with a uniformed officer, a co-pilot, who had in his hand a sheet of paper, evidently a list of passengers. He glanced at the seat number of the bespectacled offender, then at him: "Professor Sygmund Schatt?" "Sygmund spelt with a y," precised the professor. "Nothing wrong. I was merely making a professional observation."

"Keep them to yourself in future."

"I will not be silenced," said Sygmund Schatt. "Plot and scheme against me as you may."

The co-pilot went to the couple, bent towards them, and whispered something reassuring.

"You see!" said Schatt.

The pilot walked up the aisle towards Cynthia. He sat down beside her.

"A complete nut. They do cause anxiety on planes. But maybe he's harmless. He'd better be. Are you feeling lonely?"

Cynthia looked at the officer. He was good-looking, fairly young, young enough. "Just a bit," she said.

"First class is empty," said the officer. "Like to come there?"

"I don't want to—"

"Come with me," he said. "What's your name?"

"Cynthia. What's yours?"

"Tom. I'm one of the pilots. There are three of us today so far. Another's coming on at Bangkok."

"That makes me feel safe."

❄

It fell about that at Bangkok, when everyone else had got off the plane to stretch their legs for an hour and a half; the passengers had gone to walk around the departments of the Duty Free shop, buy presents "from Bangkok" of a useless nature such as dolls and silk ties, to drink coffee and other beverages with biscuits and pastries; Tom and Cynthia stayed on. They made love in a beautifully appointed cabin with real curtains in the windows—unrealistic yellow flowers on a white background. Then they talked about each other, and made love again.

"Christmas day," he said. "I'll never forget this one."

"Nor me," she said.

They had half an hour before the crew and passengers would rejoin them. One of the tankers which had refuelled the plane could be seen moving off.

Cynthia luxuriated in the washroom with its toilet waters and toothbrushes. She made herself fresh and pretty, combed her well-cut casque of dark hair. When she got back to the cabin he was returning from somewhere, looking young, smiling. He gave her a box. "Christmas present."

It contained a set of plaster Christmas crib figures, "made in China". A kneeling Virgin and St Joseph, the baby Jesus and a shoemaker with his bench, a woodcutter, an unidentifiable monk, two shepherds and two angels.

Cynthia arranged them on the table in front of her.

"Do you believe in it?" she said.

"Well, I believe in Christmas."

"Yes, I, too. It means a new life. I don't see any mother and father really kneeling beside the baby's cot worshipping it, do you?"

"No, that part's symbolic."

"These are simply lovely," she said touching her presents. "Made of real stuff, not plastic"

"Let's celebrate," he said. He disappeared and returned with a bottle of champagne.

"How expensive ..."

"Don't worry. It flows on First."

"Will you be going on duty?"

"No," he said. "I clock in tomorrow."

They made love again, high up in the air.

After that, Cynthia walked back to her former compartment. Professor Sygmund Schatt was having an argument with a hostess about his food which had apparently been pre-ordered, and now, in some way, did not come up to scratch. Cynthia sat in her old seat, and taking a postcard from the pocket in front of her, wrote to her cousin Moira. "Having a lovely time at 35,000 feet. I have started a new life. Love XX Cynthia." She then felt this former seat was part of the old life, and went back again to First.

In the night Tom came and sat beside her.

"You didn't eat much," he said.

"How did you know?"

"I noticed."

"I didn't feel up to the Christmas dinner," she said.

"Would you like something now?"

"A turkey sandwich. Let me go and ask the hostess."

"Leave it to me."

❄

Tom told her he was now in the final stages of a divorce. His wife had no doubt had a hard time of it, his job taking him away so much. But she could have studied something. She wouldn't learn, hated to learn.

And he was lonely. He asked her to marry him, and she wasn't in the least surprised. But she said, "Oh, Tom, you don't know me."

"I think I do."

"We don't know each other."

"Well, I think we should do."

She said she would think about it. She said she would cancel her plans and come to spend some time in his flat in London at Camden Town.

"I'll have my time off within three days—by the end of the week," he said.

"God, is he all right, is he reliable?" she said to herself. "Am I safe with him? Who is he?" But she was really carried away.

Around 4 a.m. she woke and found him beside her. He said, "It's Boxing day now. You're a lovely girl."

She had always imagined she was, but had always, so far, fallen timid when with men. She had experienced two brief love affairs in Australia, neither memorable. All alone in the first class compartment with Tom, high in the air—this was reality, something to be remembered, the start of a new life.

❄

"I'll give you the key of the flat," he said. "Go straight there. Nobody will disturb you. I've been sharing it with my young brother. But he's away for about six weeks I should say. In fact he's doing time. He got mixed up in a football row and he's in for grievous bodily harm and affray. Only, the bodily harm wasn't so grievous. He was just in the wrong place at the wrong time. Anyway, the flat's free for at least six weeks."

✳

At the airport, despite the early hour of ten past five in the morning, there was quite a crowd to meet the plane. Having retrieved her luggage, Cynthia pushed her trolley towards the exit. She had no expectation whatsoever that anyone would be there to meet her.

Instead, there was her father and his wife Elaine; there was her mother with her husband Bill; crowding behind them at the barrier were her brother and his girlfriend, her cousin Moira's cousin by marriage, and a few other men and women whom she did not identify, accompanied, too, by some children of about 10 to 14. In fact her whole family, known and unknown, had turned out to meet Cynthia. How had they known the hour of her arrival? She had promised, only, to ring them when she got to England. "Your cousin Moira," said her father, "told us your flight. We wanted you home, you know that."

She went first to her mother's house. It was now Boxing day but they had saved Christmas day for her arrival. All the Christmas rituals were fully observed. The tree and the presents—dozens of presents for Cynthia. Her brother and his girl with some other cousins came over for Christmas dinner.

When they came to open the presents, Cynthia brought out from her luggage a number of packages she had brought from Australia for the occasion. Among them, labelled for her brother, was a plaster Nativity set, made in China.

"What a nice one," said her brother. "One of the best I've seen, and not plastic."

"I got it in Moira's boutique," Cynthia said. "She has very special things."

She talked a lot about Australia, its marvels. Then, at tea-time, they got down to her aunt's will, of which Cynthia was an executor. Cynthia felt happy, in her element, as an executor to a will, for she was normally dreamy, not legally minded at all and now she felt the flattery of her aunt's confidence in her. The executorship gave her some sort of authority in the family. She was now arranging, too, to spend New Year with her father and his second clan.

Her brother had set out the Nativity figures on a table. "I don't know," she said, "why the mother and the father are kneeling beside the child; it seems so unreal." She didn't hear what the others said, if anything, in response to this observation. She only felt a strange stirring of memory. There was to be a flat in Camden Town, but she had no idea of the address.

"The plane stopped at Bangkok," she told them.

"Did you get off?"

"Yes, but you know you can't get out of the airport. There was a coffee bar and a lovely shop."

It was later that day when she was alone, unpacking, in her room, that she rang the airline.

"No," said a girl's voice, "I don't think there are curtains with yellow flowers in the first-class cabins. I'll have to ask. Was there any particular reason ...?"

"There was a co-pilot called Tom. Can you give me his full name please? I have an urgent message for him."

"What flight did you say?"

Cynthia told her not only the flight but her name and original seat number in Business Class.

After a long wait, the voice spoke again, "Yes, you are one of the arrivals."

"I know that," said Cynthia.

"I can't give you information about our pilots, I'm afraid. But there was no pilot on the plane called Tom … Thomas, no. The stewards in Business were Bob, Andrew, Sheila and Lilian."

"No pilot called Tom? About thirty-five, tall, brown hair. I met him. He lives in Camden Town." Cynthia gripped the phone. She looked round at the reality of the room.

"The pilots are Australian; I can tell you that but no more. I'm sorry. They're our personnel."

"It was a memorable flight. Christmas day. I'll never forget that one," said Cynthia.

"Thank you. We appreciate that," said the voice. It seemed thousands of miles away.

The Little Christmas Tree

STELLA GIBBONS

❄

Because she was tired of living in London among clever people, Miss Rhoda Harting, a reserved yet moderately successful novelist in the thirty-third year of her age, retired during one November to a cottage in Buckinghamshire. Nor did she wish to marry.

"I dislike fuss, noise, worry, and all the other accidents, which, so my friends tell me, attend the married state," she said. "I like being alone. I like my work. Why should I marry?"

"You are unnatural, Rhoda," protested her friends.

"Possibly, but at least I am cheerful," retorted Miss Harting. "Which," she added (but this was to herself), "is more than can be said of most of you."

The cottage in Buckinghamshire, which was near Great Missenden, suited her tastes. It had a double holly tree in the garden, and a well in whose dark depths she could see her own silhouette against the wintry blue sky. It stood in a lane, with long fields at the back which sloped up to a hill with a square beechwood on the summit. Halfway up the hill stood another house, Monkswell, a large, new, red house. Miss Harting used to look at this house and say contentedly, "I feel like the gardener at Monkswell. This used to be his cottage, I am told."

She furnished her cottage fastidiously with English china, English prints, chintz, and a well-equipped kitchen. For the first fortnight she played with it as though it were the dolls' house it so much resembled, but soon she began to work on a new novel, and, as everybody knows, the writing of novels does not allow time for playing at anything.

A quiet, pleasant routine, therefore, replaced her first delighted experiments.

❄

Weeks went past so quickly that she was quite surprised to receive a letter one morning beginning, "Darling Rhoda, you will come to us for Christmas, won't you, unless you have already made other plans"—and headed with an address in Kensington.

She got up from the breakfast table, where the steam from her China tea was wavering peacefully up into the air, and went over to the window and stood looking out.

"No, I shall stay here for Christmas," decided Miss Harting, after a prolonged gaze out of the window. "I shall have a chicken all to myself, and a little tree with candles and those bright, glittery balls we used to buy when we were small." She paused, in her comfortable murmuring to herself, and added contentedly, "It is really shocking. I grow more and more spinsterish every year. Something ought to be done about it. ..."

❄

Her conscience quieted, Miss Harting went shopping in Great Missenden on Christmas Eve, wandering down the rambling bright-lit High Street with a big basket slung on her arm and her bright eyes dreaming in and out of the shop windows.

The long street was packed with people, and there was a feeling of frost in the air, but no stars, only a dense, muffling bed of cloud almost touching the bare beechwoods on the hidden hills all round the little town. In the butchers' shops the dangling turkeys were tied up with red ribbon, and hares were decorated with spiked bunches of holly and moon-mistletoe, and out of the warm caverns of the two wireless and gramophone shops poured rich, blaring music.

"Seasonable weather, madam," said the poulterer who tied up Miss Harting's small but fat chicken.

"Going to be a regular old-fashioned Christmas, Miss," said the old lady wrapped in a shawl like a thick, blacky-green fishing net, who packed up the silver glass balls and red and green lemons of fairy-glass that Miss Harting had chosen for her Christmas tree.

The old lady looked across at her with something more than professional interest, and enquired civilly:

"Was you wanting them for a Christmas tree of your own, Miss?"

"Yes," murmured Miss Harting.

"Ah! Nephews and nieces coming down from London perhaps?"

"Well—no," confessed her customer.

"Not your own little ones? Excuse me askin', but you can usually tell. I shouldn't have thought ... Well, there now, I'm sure I beg your pardon. I oughtn't to have said that. Here's the toys, Miss. A happy Christmas to you."

"Er—thank you. The same to you. Good evening."

Miss Harting escaped, aware that the old lady, far from being embarrassed by her mistake, was taking her in from head to feet with lively, curious eyes and thought her a queer one. But Miss Harting was sure that her wildest guesses at the reason why the toys had been bought would come nowhere near the truth. In the circles in which the old lady's tubby person rotated, unmarried females did not buy Christmas trees, decorate them and gloat over them in solitude, however natural such a proceeding might seem in Chelsea.

❄

Perhaps it was this breath of commonsense from the world of unimaginative millions that made Miss Harting feel a little depressed as she got down from the Amersham 'bus at the cross roads, and set out along the ringing frosty road to walk the last mile to her cottage. Her basket hung heavily on her arm. She was hungry. She did not feel in the mood for revelling in the bright, miniature prettiness of her Christmas tree. She almost wished she had gone to Kensington, as her friends had proposed. "Good gracious, this will never do," muttered Miss Harting, unlocking her front door. "In the New Year I will go up to London and see people, and invite Lucy or Hans Carter or somebody to come down and stay with me."

When she had eaten her supper, however, she felt better; and began to enjoy bedding the shapely little tree into a flower-pot and fastening the glass bells and lemons on to the tips of its branches. She stood it in the sitting-room window, with the curtains pulled back, when it was ready, and could not resist lighting its tipsy green and white candles, just to see what it would look like.

Oh! the soft light shining round the candles and falling down between the dark green branches! How pretty it was!

She stood for perhaps five minutes dreaming in front of it, in a silence unbroken except by the noise of a car that droned past along the unfrequented lane at the foot of her front garden.

Every year, ever since she could remember, she had had a Christmas tree, either bought for her by her parents, when they were alive, or by herself, with her own money. This year, it was as beautiful and as satisfying as ever.

Yet ... was it? While she stood looking at it, she remembered the old lady in the little shop. The thought drifted into her mind that hers was a lonely, not to say self-conscious, way of enjoying a Christmas tree. She dismissed the thought impatiently, extinguished the little candles, and spent the rest of the evening profitably at work on her book.

❄

In the night the snow came. She awoke on Christmas morning in that unmistakable light, coming up from the earth and shining between her curtains. All her loneliness and depression had gone. She felt as happy and excited as though she were going to a feast.

But when she had nibbled her breakfast, played Debussy's *Footsteps in the Snow* twice on the gramophone, stuffed her chicken and glanced more than once at her Christmas tree, whose bells glittered darkly against the snow, she found herself trying to feel happy, rather than feeling happy. It was eleven o'clock. The noise of bells was stealing in soft claps of sound on the snow-wind. She suddenly faced the fact that she was both lonely and bored; that eleven more empty hours yawned endlessly in front of her, and that she could do nothing to stop their approach and departure.

It was just at this moment, as she stood staring down at her fingers still greasy with chicken-stuffing, that there came a knock at the front door.

Miss Harting gave a great start.

"Oh!" she thought, with a rush of relief, "perhaps it's some one come down from London to see me!" and she hurried out to the door.

But when she opened the door she saw no gay, familiar face from London. A little girl, wearing a red beret, stood on the doorstep, squarely yet somehow in a pose that suggested she might dash away in a second, looking up with large dark eyes into Miss Harting's surprised face. Two smaller children, in the same tiptoe pose, lurked in the background.

"Good morning," said the red beret loudly and politely. "We are very sorry to trouble you, but please may we take shelter in your house?"

"Shelter?" said Miss Harting, still getting over her silly disappointment that it was not a delightful visitor from London; and perhaps she spoke a little curtly. "Because of the snow, do you mean? But—" she glanced up at the sky—"it isn't snowing. What's the matter? Are your feet wet or something?" (No one but a nieceless spinster would have asked such a question of a little girl on a snowy morning.)

"No, thank you," said the red beret politely. "It isn't that sort of shelter, and our feet are quite dry, thank you very much. But, you see, it is rather necessary that we should take shelter, because"—she looked up candidly into Miss Harting's eyes—"some one is coming after us, and we want to hide."

She glanced round at the two smaller figures, who both nodded violently as though she had pulled a string.

"Who's after you?" asked Miss Harting, startled. "Are you playing a game?"

"Oh, no. *Truly*, it isn't a game. It's rather serious, as a matter of fact. You see, we have a cruel step-mother, and she said we weren't to have a proper Christmas tree this year, and Jane and Harry— these are Jane and Harry," (jerking them forward and muttering, "Say-how-do-you-do," which they did, like two polite wool-clad parrots)—"cried rather a lot—"

"I didn't, Judy. 'At's a story!" interrupted the other little girl flatly at this point in the narrative. "And if you say I cried like a baby, I shall tell—you-know-what!"

"Oh, well then, perhaps you didn't cry quite as much as Harry," conceded the red beret, darting a lightning grimace at her, laden with menace. "But Harry cried all night. So we got up very early this morning, before it was light, and took some gingerbreads and hid in the woods until it got light, and then we ran down—I mean we walked a long way in the woods, until we saw your house, and as we were rather hung—I mean, we thought we would ask if we might take shelter here until our step-mother had stopped looking for us. That's what we thought, isn't it?" appealing imperiously to the woolly parrots.

"Yes, we liked your house because it was so *little*," said Jane, accompanying her compliment by a smile of such specious yet goblin charm that Rhoda's heart contracted strangely.

Here Harry, who had been staring at her face, remarked "Absolutely snow," and pointed to the distant fields. He added, after another prolonged stare, "You do look funny," and began to run slowly up and down the path with his hands at his sides, puffing like an engine.

"Harry! That's rude!" cried the red beret, darting down on him. "You mustn't mind him, please. He's only four and doesn't understand things properly yet. Besides, he isn't our brother. He's only a cousin."

A pause followed; an awkward pause. The red beret and the woolly Jane gazed up into Miss Harting's face, too polite to put their request again into words, but with eyes full of pleading and hope.

She did not know quite what to do. She did not, of course, believe a word of the red beret's fantastic story. The red beret, with her over-persuasive eyes and tongue, had betrayed herself with her first sentence as one of those incurable romancers who are doomed never to be believed.

"She will probably earn a large income one day by writing best-sellers," thought Miss Harting, who was now handicapped by having to struggle with the pangs of violent love at first sight. It did not seem at all shocking to her that the red beret should tell lies, but she did wonder very much whether the red beret had a mother, and if so, did she know of the daughter's capacities for inventing? It seemed to Miss Harting that these three needed looking after. In spite of their educated enunciation, their warm clothes and pretty manners, they had a lost look about them.

But, if they felt lost, why in the name of Father Christmas himself should they choose her unromantic doorstep to be lost on? Taking another long look at their anxious faces, she sighed, and gave it up.

She said, cautiously (but a curious warm feeling of happiness began to invade her), "Well, come in by all means, if your step-mother is as bad as all that. You can stay until you're warm, anyway. Jane—that is your name, isn't it?—is beginning to look blue. Er—you can see my Christmas tree, too, if that would amuse you."

❄

The two faces changed with incredible speed. They smiled, but Rhoda felt that was a smile of triumph, of success achieved, rather than one of gratitude. She was sure that only prudence prevented the red beret from saying to Jane, "There you are, clever! I told you so!" and she became more than ever puzzled.

"Oh, thank you *very* much—" gushed the red beret.

"*Vewy* much," came Jane's slower, fatter voice, in dutiful diminuendo.

"I'm afraid there are no presents on it," warned Rhoda, opening the kitchen door. But there was no need for apologies. The three paused on the threshold, staring at the little tree, their faces solemn with pleasure.

"Oh, isn't it *pretty!* It's so *little!* It's like those little ones we saw growing near Barnet," said the red beret. "Daddy told us they were going to be Christmas trees when they got bigger. Oh, what pretty little bell-things. Oh, look Jane, a norange! all made of glass!"

"Pretty!" said Jane, intensely. "It's the littlest tree I ever saw. May I touch it? Who is it for?"

"Er—it's for you," said Rhoda, feeling very queer indeed. Yet they were all warmly-clad, all well-fed and healthy. It was ridiculous to feel inclined to cry.

The three faces, incredulous, were lifted to hers.

"For us? Oo! Really? Can we play with it? Can I have the little lemon thing? Can we light those little cangles ourselves?"

"After lunch," said Rhoda, who had suddenly become so full of bustling happiness that she could not keep still, and she began to tie on her white cooking overall with unnecessary energy.

"Is that your lunch cooking?" asked Jane, looking round the kitchen with polite interest. "It smells nice."

"Jane!" warned the red beret. She glanced appealingly at Miss Harting. "Jane's only six. I'm nearly nine. Jane's rather rude sometimes. She's still fairly little, you see."

"I suppose your cruel step-mother hasn't much time to teach Jane manners, either," said Miss Harting drily. She was used, of course, to the type of grown-up person to whom ironical conversation is natural.

But in this case irony would not do. She realized it at once with extreme contrition, as the red beret stared up at her, wounded and rather frightened by her tone. She knelt down in front of her suddenly, and murmured, beginning to unbutton the reefer coat:

"What's your name? Mine's Rhoda Harting. Let me help you off with your coat. Will you please all stay and have lunch?"

"Oo, hooray! I'm so hungry," shouted Harry, who had been poking at the bells on the Christmas tree and exchanging hoarse whispers with Jane.

"Thank you very much. We should like to. As a matter of fact, we are rather hun'gry. I'm Juliet Woodhouse, but I'm us'herly called Judy," said the red beret.

Rhoda carefully folded the little coat and put it on her Welsh dresser. "I must cook potatoes," she said.

"Oh, let me help," said Judy, eagerly. "May I fill the saucepan? Where is it?"

"We have maids at home to cook our lunch," said Jane, mildly, watching these preparations. She had put her hat and coat on a chair, and now looked more than ever like a gnome. She had the shortest face and nose Rhoda had ever seen, framed in a streaked straw bob. Harry was red and round, and his voice was strident. He said little, but what he said was to the point.

"Is Jane really your sister? You are so fair and she is so dark—like Snow White and Rosy Red. Where do you live?" asked Rhoda, half an hour later, as she and Judy were laying the cloth. Her curiosity refused to lie down and behave politely, even though she was the hostess.

"Yes, she is, really. Oh, we live a long way away from here. I don't expect you would know it," said Judy, vague as the organizer of a charity matinée. "Look! Jane has dropped her apple core on your pretty rug. Do you mind?"

"No," said Rhoda. Nor did she. The kitchen smelled of roast chicken, burnt fir branches (for they had, of course, lit the candles), hot wax, and raspberry jam. Rhoda, putting plates on the table, wondered if it were really only an hour ago that she had felt lonely and bored.

Judy was darting about the kitchen like an elfin actress, fastidiously selecting forks, making her fingers hover undecidedly over spoons and glasses, shaking her dark hair back from her face. Rhoda, watching rather sadly, thought she had seldom seen prettier or more self-conscious actions. She wondered more and more what Judy's mother could be like.

❄

Amid a pleasant scramble Rhoda got the three of them seated at her kitchen table. The white snowlight lit up the two absorbed, innocent faces turned towards the window, and made a background for Judy's dark head. Rhoda looked round at the three of them, blessing the chance that had brought them to her doorstep on Christmas morning, and wondered, as she minced chicken for Harry, whether they would stay the night, who they could possibly be, and—a more serious thought—whether some poor mother was spending a terrible Christmas Day somewhere looking for them.

Yet, beyond her one question to Judy and Judy's casual avoidance of a direct answer, she could not bring herself to ask them bluntly who they were and where they lived. After all, they were her guests, though self-invited. They had thrown themselves on her mercy. She felt she could not take advantage of their childish state and behave to them as a grown up person. She had to meet them on their own ground. It was delightful to have them at her table, filling her carefully-furnished kitchen with the noise of their merry voices and their polite laughter at her jokes and giggles at their own.

"Is this turkey?" demanded Harry, presently.

"No, darling; it's chicken. Don't you like it?" asked foolish Rhoda, anxiously.

"No. More please," said Harry.

"You are silly, Harry," said Jane. "Saying 'No, you don't like it,' and then asking if you can have some more. Isn't he silly, Judy?"

"He's only little," from Judy, patronizingly. "Don't worry him."

"If we were at home we *should* be having turkey, but this is much nicer," said Jane. Judy's foot stealthily knocked against hers under the table.

"No, Jane, we shouldn't be having turkey. Our step-mother wouldn't let us, would she?"

"No, I s'pose she wouldn't. She's very crool," said Jane, influenced by the kick and by Judy's meaning nod.

Rhoda had decided that it was not quite fair to show her disbelief in the step-mother legend, so she joined in politely with—

"How disgraceful. Doesn't she even let you have turkey on Christmas Day?"

"No. She's *awful*, isn't she, Jane?"

"Yes, simply *awful*," agreed Jane. "Isn't she awful, Harry?" suddenly giggling into Harry's neck.

"Don't. Old man wiv scizzors," said Harry, whose mind was evidently still at work on the pictures in the Nonsuch Blake at which he had been looking.

After Rhoda's little Christmas pudding had been greeted with cries of delight, "Oh, isn't it *little!*" "It's the littlest pudding I ever saw!" and eaten, Rhoda had to confess that she had no crystallized fruits or crackers, so they must light the Christmas tree again and then play games.

This suggestion was welcomed with rapture, and Judy, as the eldest, lit six of the little candles, and Jane and Harry lit the remaining six. Rhoda lifted Harry up, putting her cheek for a moment against his warm head.

❄

Darkness was beginning to fall, and the snow gleamed in its own ghostly light under the deepening blue of the sky.

Now the Christmas tree was all alight, the candles burnt still and pointed against the green branches. Three little faces were turned up to the tree, with the candlelight making aureoles round their hair. They were silent, staring up at the beautiful, half-despoiled little tree.

"Oh," thought Rhoda, looking at them, "that's how it should have been last night! It looks *right* now, somehow. Darlings ... how glad I am I had it here, ready for them ..."

The entranced pause was broken by a loud knock at the front door.

Judy flew round, her eyes dilated.

"Who's that? That's some one come for us! We won't go! Tell them to go away! I *like* being here! I won't go home!"

"It's Daddy," said Jane, resignedly. "I knew they'd find us, Judy. I told you so."

"I lit free cangles by myself," said Harry, holding up the stump of his match.

Rhoda, smoothing her fingers across her straying hair, with a distressed look on her face, was halfway to the door when Judy came flying down the passage after her, and locked her arms round her waist.

"Don't tell! Don't tell about the step-mother," she implored in a frightened whisper, lifting a white, distorted little face in the dusk. "I made it up. I made it all up, and Daddy said I was never to make anything up again—*ever*. We saw your little tree all lit up in the window last night, when Daddy was driving us back from London. We wanted to see your little tree. We've never had a *little* tree at home. Everything's so *big*. It's horrid. We haven't got any mother— Jane and I haven't. Promise you won't tell about the step-mother? Promise—promise!"

Her grip tightened round Rhoda's waist, her eyes, enormous with terror, stared up imploringly. The knock was repeated, twice, louder, and impatiently.

"No, darling. Of course I won't tell. I promise faithfully, Judy. Now let me go, darling. Take your arms away, there's a dear little girl!"

Judy darted her a look of passionate gratitude and flew back to the kitchen. Rhoda, her heart beating unpleasantly, opened the front door.

The man standing there saw a tall woman, silhouetted against a candle-lit passage, and noticed how white her hand was against the door handle. He took off his hat.

"Good evening. I'm sorry to disturb you, but I suppose you don't happen to have seen my two daughters and my nephew, do you? My name's Woodhouse. We live up at Monkswell. The three of them have been missing since just after breakfast, and their aunt's nearly frantic. The eldest girl's got on a red tam-o'-shanter, I believe—"

"Yes. They're in here, with me," Rhoda interrupted the uncultured but pleasant voice, and stood aside to let him enter. Over his big shoulder she saw a long saloon car blocking the lane at the foot of her garden. "Won't you come in? I'm so sorry ... you must have had a terrible day. They've been quite safe, of course, but I couldn't get out of them where they lived or to whom they belonged."

"Ah! Judy romancing again, I suppose."

He came forward into the candlelight. Tall, middle-aged, prosperous; clever eyes, weak mouth, good chin. Not a gentleman. I like him. Rhoda's usually well-ordered thoughts raced confusedly.

"Judy should make her fortune out of writing best-sellers when she is older," she said, stopping just outside the kitchen door, which had been carefully closed by the strategists within; "but I am sure you will not scold her for romancing to-day. She is very penitent, and they have all been so good and so happy."

"They had a Christmas tree the size of a house at home, and any amount of presents—all the usual things children expect at Christmas," he interrupted, roughly. "Why should they come down here, bothering you? It's intolerable. They get more out of hand every week. Their aunt can't do anything with them, and I'm away all day, and most week-ends. Especially Judy. She's the most shameless little liar—And yet, you know," his irritable expression suddenly changed, and his face became cautious, intelligent, as though he were weighing a problem—"it isn't just lying. It's something quite different. She seems to need it, somehow. I haven't the heart to be very hard on her. I'm worried about Judy. She wants some one to look after her."

He paused. "Their mother died when Jane was born. It hasn't been a particularly cheerful household since. I suppose they both need looking after properly."

There was another pause.

❄️

In that pause, filled with the soft light of the candles now burning low on the little Christmas tree, and with silence, his unsatisfied, clever eyes took in the fineness of Rhoda's ringless hands, the subtle and tender modelling of her mouth, and the irony which looked out like an armed sentinel from her eyes.

But it seemed to him a sentinel who might be persuaded, one day, to lay aside its weapon.

"Well," said Rhoda, lightly, at last, "Shall we go in to the children?"

The Christmas Present

RICHMAL CROMPTON

❄

Mary Clay looked out of the window of the old farmhouse. The view was dreary enough—hill and field and woodland, bare, colourless, mist-covered—with no other houses in sight. She had never been a woman to crave for company. She liked sewing. She was passionately fond of reading. She was not fond of talking. Probably she could have been very happy at Cromb Farm—alone. Before her marriage she had looked forward to the long evenings with her sewing and reading. She knew that she would be busy enough in the day, for the farmhouse was old and rambling, and she was to have no help in the housework. But she looked forward to quiet, peaceful, lamplit evenings; and only lately, after ten years of married life, had she reluctantly given up the hope of them. For peace was far enough from the old farm kitchen in the evening. It was driven away by John Clay's loud voice, raised always in orders or complaints, or in the stumbling, incoherent reading aloud of his newspaper.

Mary was a silent woman herself and a lover of silence. But John liked to hear the sound of his voice; he liked to shout at her; to call for her from one room to another; above all, he liked to hear his voice reading the paper out loud to her in the evening. She dreaded that most of all. It had lately seemed to jar on her nerves till she felt she must scream aloud. His voice going on and on, raucous and sing-song, became unspeakably irritating. His "Mary!" summoning her from her household work to wherever he happened to be, his "Get my slippers," or "Bring me my pipe," exasperated her almost to the point of rebellion. "Get your own slippers" had trembled on her lips, but had never passed them, for she was a woman who could not bear anger. Noise of any kind appalled her.

She had borne it for ten years, so surely she could go on with it. Yet today, as she gazed hopelessly at the wintry country side, she became acutely conscious that she could not go on with it. Something must happen. Yet what was there that could happen?

It was Christmas next week. She smiled ironically at the thought. Then she noticed the figure of her husband coming up the road. He came in at the gate and round to the side-door.

"Mary!"

She went slowly in answer to the summons. He held a letter in his hand.

"Met the postman," he said. "From your aunt."

She opened the letter and read in silence. Both of them knew quite well what it contained.

"She wants us to go over for Christmas again," said Mary.

He began to grumble.

"She's as deaf as a post. She's 'most as deaf as her mother was. She ought to know better than to ask folks over when she can't hear a word any one says."

Mary said nothing. He always grumbled about the invitation at first, but really he wanted to go. He liked to talk with her uncle.

He liked the change of going down to the village for a few days and hearing all its gossip. He could quite well leave the farm to the "hands" for that time.

The Crewe deafness was proverbial. Mary's great-grandmother had gone stone deaf at the age of thirty-five; her daughter had inherited the affliction and her grand-daughter, the aunt with whom Mary had spent her childhood, had inherited it also at exactly the same age.

"All right," he said at last, grudgingly, as though in answer to her silence, "we'd better go. Write and say we'll go."

❄

It was Christmas Eve. They were in the kitchen of her uncle's farmhouse. The deaf old woman sat in her chair by the fire knitting. Upon her sunken face there was a curious sardonic smile that was her habitual expression. The two men stood in the doorway. Mary sat at the table looking aimlessly out of the window. Outside, the snow fell in blinding showers. Inside, the fire gleamed on to the copper pots and pans, the crockery on the old oak dresser, the hams hanging from the ceiling.

Suddenly James turned.

"Jane!" he said.

The deaf woman never stirred.

"Jane!"

Still there was no response upon the enigmatic old face by the fireside.

"Jane!"

She turned slightly towards the voice.

"Get them photos from upstairs to show John," he bawled.

"What about boats?" she said.

"Photos!" roared her husband.

"Coats?" she quavered.

Mary looked from one to the other. The man made a gesture of irritation and went from the room.

He came back with a pile of picture postcards in his hand.

"It's quicker to do a thing oneself," he grumbled. "They're what my brother sent from Switzerland, where he's working now. It's a fine land, to judge from the views of it."

John took them from his hand. "She gets worse?" he said nodding towards the old woman.

She was sitting gazing at the fire, her lips curved into a curious smile.

Her husband shrugged his shoulders. "Aye. She's nigh as bad as her mother was."

"And her grandmother."

"Aye. It takes longer to tell her to do something than to do it myself. And deaf folks get a bit stupid, too. Can't see what you mean. They're best let alone."

The other man nodded and lit his pipe. Then James opened the door.

"The snow's stopped," he said. "Shall we go to the end of the village and back?"

The other nodded, and took his cap from behind the door. A gust of cold air filled the room as they went out.

Mary took a paper-backed book from the table and came over to the fireplace.

"Mary!"

She started. It was not the sharp, querulous voice of the deaf old woman. It was more like the voice of the young aunt whom Mary remembered in childhood. The old woman was leaning forward, looking at her intently.

"Mary! A happy Christmas to 'ee."

And, as if in spite of herself, Mary answered in her ordinary low tones.

"The same to you, auntie."

"Thank 'ee. Thank 'ee."

Mary gasped.

"Aunt! Can you hear me speaking like this?"

The old woman laughed, silently, rocking to and fro in her chair as if with pent-up merriment of years.

"Yes, I can hear 'ee, child. I've allus heard 'ee."

Mary clasped her hand eagerly.

"Then—you're cured, Aunt—"

"Ay. I'm cured as far as there was ever anything to be cured."

"You—?"

"I was never deaf, child, nor never will be, please God. I've took you all in fine."

Mary stood up in bewilderment.

"You? Never deaf?"

The old woman chuckled again.

"No, nor my mother—nor her mother neither."

Mary shrank back from her.

"I—I don't know what you mean," she said, unsteadily. "Have you been—pretending?"

"I'll make you a Christmas present of it, dearie," said the old woman. "My mother made me a Christmas present of it when I was your age, and her mother made her one. I haven't a lass of my own to give it to, so I give it to you. It can come on quite sudden like, if you want it, and then you can hear what you choose and not hear what you choose. Do you see?" She leant nearer and whispered, "You're shut out of it all—of having to fetch and carry for 'em, answer their daft questions and run their errands like a dog. I've watched you, my lass. You don't get much peace, do you?"

Mary was trembling.

"Oh, I don't know what to think," she said. "I—I couldn't do it."

"Do what you like," said the old woman. "Take it as a present, anyways—the Crewe deafness for a Christmas present," she chuckled. "Use it or not as you like. You'll find it main amusin', anyways."

And into the old face there came again that curious smile as if she carried in her heart some jest fit for the gods on Olympus.

The door opened suddenly with another gust of cold air, and the two men came in again, covered with fine snow.

"I—I'll not do it," whispered Mary, trembling.

"We didn't get far. It's coming on again," remarked John, hanging up his cap.

The old woman rose and began to lay the supper, silently and deftly, moving from cupboard to table without looking up. Mary sat by the fire, motionless and speechless, her eyes fixed on the glowing coals.

"Any signs o' the deafness in her?" whispered James, looking towards Mary. "It come on my wife jus' when she was that age."

"Aye, so I've heered."

Then he said loudly, "Mary!"

A faint pink colour came into her cheeks, but she did not show by look or movement that she had heard. James looked significantly at her husband.

The old woman stood still for a minute with a cup in each hand and smiled her slow, subtle smile.

Christmas Bread

KATHLEEN NORRIS

"But what time will your operation be over, mother?"

A silence. The surgeon opened three letters, looked at them, tore them in two, cast them aside, glanced at her newspaper, glanced at her coffee cup, and took a casual sip of the smoking liquid. But she did not answer.

"If you were thr-r-rough at 'leven o'clock—" Merle began again hopefully. She paid some attention to consonants, because until recently she had called through "froo," and she was anxious to seem grown-up. "I could go to the hospital with Miss Frothingham," she suggested, "and wait for you?"

"I thought Miss Frothingham was going to take you to Mrs. Winchester's?" Doctor madison countered in surprise, at last giving a partial attention to her little daughter. "Don't you want to spend Christmas Day with little Betty?" she went on, easily, half-absently. "It seems to me that is a very nice plan—straighten your shoulders dear. It seems to me that it was extremely nice of Mrs. Winchester to want you to come. Most people want only their own families on Christmas Day!"

She was paying small heed to her own words. "That band really did straighten her teeth," she was thinking. "I must remind Miss Frothingham to order some more of the little smocks; she doesn't look half so well in the blue-jacket blouses. How like George she is growing! ... What did you say, Merle?" she added, realising that the child's plaintive voice was lingering still in the air.

"I said that *I* would like my own family, too, on Christmas," the child repeated, half-daring, half-uncertain.

"Ring the bell, dear," her mother said from the newspaper.

"I wish I didn't know what you were going to give me for Christmas, mother."

"You what?"

"I wish I didn't know what you were going to give me!"

Silence.

"For Christmas, you know?" Merle prompted. "I know your present. I love to have a little desk all my own. It's just like Betty's, too, only prettier. But I would drather have it a surprise, and run down Christmas morning to see what it was!"

"Don't say 'drather,' dear."

"Rather." With the gold spoon, Merle made a river through her cream of wheat in the monogrammed gold bowl and watched the cream rivers flood together. "What interests you in the paper, mother?" she asked politely.

"Why, they are going to have the convention in California next summer," her mother said.

"And shall you go, mother?"

"Oh, I think so! Perhaps you and Miss Frothingham will go with me."

"To hotels?"

"I suppose so."

Merle sighed. She did not like large strange hotels. "Mother, doesn't it seem funny to you that a patient would have his operation on Christmas Day? Couldn't he have it to-morrow, or wait till Wednesday?"

The doctor's fine mouth twitched at the corners. "Poor fellow, they only get him here to-morrow, Merle, Christmas morning. And they tell me there is no time to lose."

Tears came into the little girl's eyes. "It doesn't seem—much—like Christmas," she murmured under her breath. "To have you in the surgery all morning, and me with the Winchesters, that aren't my relations at all—"

"Tell me exactly what you had planned to do, Merle," her mother suggested reasonably. "Perhaps we can manage it for some other day. What did you specially want to do?"

The kindly, logical tone was that of the surgeon used to matters no less vital than life and death. Merle raised her round, childish eyes to her mother's pleasant, keen ones. Then with a great sigh she returned to the golden bowl and spoon. Nothing more was said until Lizzie came in for the orders.

"Dear me, I miss Miss Frothingham!" said Doctor Madison then. "Tell Ada to use her own judgment, Lizzie. Tell her—you might have chicken again. That doesn't spoil, in case I'm late."

"You wouldn't have a turkey, Doctor? To-morrow's Christmas, you know."

"Well—if Ada thinks so. I don't particularly care for turkey—yes, we may as well have a turkey. But no pudding, and above all, no mince-pie, Lizzie. Have something simple—prune whip, apple-sauce. I don't care! Merle will be with the Winchesters all day, and she'll need only a light supper. If there are any telephone calls, I'm at the hospital. Miss Frothingham will be back this afternoon."

Then she was gone, and there was a long lonely day ahead of her small daughter. But Merle was accustomed to them. She went into the kitchen and watched Ada and Ada's friend, Mrs. Catawba Hercules, until Miss Watson came. Then she had a music lesson, and a French lesson, and after lunch she posted herself at a front window to watch the streets and wait for pretty Miss Frothingham, who filled the double post of secretary and governess, and who had gone home yesterday to her sister's house for a Christmas visit.

Outside was Christmas weather. All morning the streets had been bare and dark, and swept with menacing winds that hurried and buffeted the marketing and shopping women. But at noon the leaden sky had turned darker and darker, and crept lower and lower, and, as Merle watched, the first timid snowflakes began to flutter whitely against the general greyness.

Then there was scurrying and laughter in the streets, bundles dampened, boys shouting and running, merry faces, rouged by the pure, soft cold. The shabby, leather-sheathed doors of St. Martin's, opposite Merle's window, creaked and swung under the touch of wet, gloved hands. Merle could see the Christmas-trees and the boxed oranges outside the State Street groceries coated with eider-down; naked gardens and fences and bare trees everywhere grew muffled and feathered and lovely. In the early twilight the whole happy town echoed with bells and horns and the clanking of snow-shovels.

By this time Miss Frothingham was back again, and was helping Merle into the picturesque black velvet with the deep lace collar.

Merle, sputtering through the blue embroidered cloth, while her face was being washed, asked how Miss Frothingham's little niece had liked her doll.

"Oh, my dear, she doesn't get it until she comes downstairs to-morrow morning, of course!"

"Will she be excited?" Merle asked, excited herself.

"She'll be perfectly frantic! I see that your mother's present came."

"My desk. It came last night. I moved all my things into it to-day," Merle said. "It doesn't feel much like Christmas when a person gets their presents two days before." she observed.

"His presents. Her presents," corrected the governess.

"Her presents. Will your sister's little girls have a tree?"

"Oh my, yes! It's a gorgeous tree!"

"And did you see my cousins while you were there?"

Miss Frothingham nodded. Her married sister lived next to Doctor Madison's brother, a struggling young engineer with a small family, in a certain not-too-fashionable suburb. There had been a difference of opinion regarding a legacy, between the physician and her brother some years earlier, and a long silence had ensued, hut Merle took a lively interest in the little cousins of whom she had only a hazy and wistful memory, and her mother had no objection to an occasional mention of them.

"I saw Rawley—that's the second little boy—playing with my niece," Miss Frothingham said. "And I saw Tommy—he's older than you—taking care of the baby. I think he was going to the grocery for his mother; he was wheeling the baby very carefully. But I think those children are going to have a pretty sad Christmas because their daddy is very sick, you know. and they all had whooping-cough, and I think their mother is too tired to know whether it's Christmas or Fourth of July!"

"Maybe their father's going to die like my father," Merle suggested stoically. "I guess they won't hang up their stockings," she added suddenly.

For it had been reported that this was their custom, and Merle liked to lie awake in her little bed, warm and cosy on a winter night, and think thrillingly of what it would be to explore a bulging and lumpy stocking of her own.

Miss Frothingham looked doubtful. "I don't suppose they will!" she opined.

Merle was shocked. "Will they cry?"

"I don't suppose so. My sister says they're extremely good children and will do anything to help their mother."

"Maybe they'll hang them up anyway, and they'll be empty?" Merle said, wide-eyed.

But the governess had lost interest in the subject, as grown-ups so often and so maddeningly did, and was manicuring her pretty nails, and humming, so Merle had to abandon it for the moment.

However, she thought about it continually, and after dinner she said suddenly and daringly to her mother:

"The Rutledge children's father is sick, and they aren't going to hang up their stockings! Miss Frothingham said so!"

When this was said, she and Miss Frothingham and her mother were all in the attic. Merle had not been there for weeks, nor her mother for months, and it was enchanting to the child to find herself bustling about so unexpectedly in this exciting atmosphere, which, if it was not typically Christmassy, was at least unusual. It had come about suddenly, as did much that affected her mother's movements.

The doctor had arrived home at half-past four, and Miss Frothingham had lost no time in reminding her that the promised bundle for the New Year's rummage sale for some charity was to have been ready this evening. Doctor Madison had said—did she remember?—that she had any amount of old clothing to dispose of.

"Oh, that attic is full of it!" Merle's mother had said, wearily. "You know this was my grandmother's house, and goodness only knows the rubbish that is up there! I've meant to get at it all some time—I couldn't do it in her lifetime. What time is it? Suppose we go up there and get a start?"

There was twilight in the attic, and outside the dormer windows the snow was falling—falling. Merle performed a little pirouette of sheer ecstasy when they mounted the stairs. Her mother lighted the lights in a business-like fashion.

"Here, take this—take this—take this!" she began to say carelessly, picking one garment after another from the low row of ghostly forms dangling against the eaves. "Mr. Madison's army coats—"

"But, Mrs. Madison, this is beautiful beaver on this suit—yards of it!"

"Take it—take it!" Merle's equable mother said feverishly, almost irritably. "Here, I shall never wear this fur-coat again, and all these hats—I suppose those plumes are worth something!"

She was an energetic, restless creature. The hard work strangely calmed her, and just before dinner she was settling down to it almost with enjoyment. The summons to the meal annoyed her.

"Suppose we come back to it and make a thorough job?" she suggested.

Merle's heart leaped for joy.

"But you ought to be in bed, Kiddie," her mother said, not ungently, when dinner was over.

"Oh, mother, please! It's Christmas Eve!" Merle begged, with all the force of her agonised eight years.

So here they all were again, and the snow was still falling outside, and the electric lights on their swinging cords were sending an eerie light over the miscellaneous shapes and contours of the attic, now making the shadow of an old what-not rush across the floor with startling vitality, now plunging the gloomy eaves behind Merle into alarming darkness.

Pyramids of books were on the floor, magazines tied in sixes with pink cord, curtains, rugs, beds, heaped mattresses, trunks, boxes, the usual wheel-chair and the usual crutch—all the significant, gathered driftwood of sixty years of living was strewn and packed and heaped and hung about.

"Here, here's a wonderful patent preserving kettle, do you suppose they could use that? And what about these four terrible patent rockers?"

"Oh, Mrs. Madison, I imagine they would be only too delighted! Their idea is to open a regular store, you know, and make the sale permanent. But ought you—"

"I ought to have done it years before! But Doctor Madison—" His widow's breast rose on a sharp sigh; she lost the words for a second. "Doctor Madison and I never lived here, you know," she resumed. "And I stayed abroad for years after his death, when Merle was a baby. And for a long time I was like a person dazed—" She stopped.

"I had my work." she resumed, after a pause. "It saved my reason, I think. Perhaps—perhaps I went into it too hard. But I had to have—to do—something! My grandparents died and left me this place and the Beachaways place, but I've had no time for housekeeping!"

"I should think not, indeed!" Miss Frothingham said, timidly respectful.

Those fingers, that could cleave so neatly into the very stronghold of life, that could touch so boldly hearts that still pulsated and lungs that still were fanned by breath, were they to count silver spoons and quilt-comforters?

The governess felt a little impressed; even a little touched. She did not often see her employer in this mood. Kind, just, reasonable, interested, capable, good, Doctor Madison always was. But this was something more.

"I had no intention of becoming rich, of being—successful!" the older woman added presently, in a dreamy tone. She was sitting with the great spread of a brocaded robe across her knee. Her eyes were absent.

"All the more fun!" Miss Frothingham said youthfully.

"I was alone—" Mary Madison said drearily and quietly, in a low tone, as if to herself. And in the three words the younger caught a glimpse of all the tragedy and loneliness of widowhood. "Doctor Madison was so wise," she began again. "I've always thought that if he had lived my life would have been different."

"You lost your parents, I know, and were you an only child?" Miss Frothingham ventured, after a respectful silence. But immediately the scarlet, apologetic colour flooded her face, and she added hastily: "I beg your pardon! Of course I knew that you have a brother—I know Mr. Rutledge and his wife!"

"Yes, I have a brother," the doctor answered, rousing, and

beginning briskly to assort and segregate again. The tone chilled her companion, and there was a pause.

"Your brother is Tommy's and Rawley's and the baby's father," Merle broke it by announcing flatly.

Her mother looked at her with an indulgent half-smile. She usually regarded Merle much as an amused stranger might have done; the odd little black-eyed, black-maned child who was always curling herself into corners about the house. Merle was going to be pretty, her mother thought to-night, in satisfaction. Her little face was blazing, her eyes shone, and she had pulled over her dishevelled curls a fantastic tissue-paper cap of autumn leaves left from some long-ago Hallowe'en frolic her mother could only half-remember.

"What do you know about them?" she asked good-naturedly. "You never saw them!"

"You told me once about them, when I was a teenty little girl," Merle reminded her. "When we were in the cemetery you did. And Miss Frothingham told me."

"So there's a third child?" Doctor Madison asked, musing. Miss Frothingham nodded.

"A gorgeous boy. The handsomest baby I ever saw!—John," she said.

"John was my father's name. Sad, isn't it?" Doctor Madison asked, after a silence, during which she had folded the brocade and added it to the heap.

"A costumier would buy lots of this just as it stands," Miss Frothingham murmured by way of answer.

"I mean when families quarrel," persisted the doctor.

"Oh, I think it is very sad!" the secretary said fervently.

"We were inseparable, as children," Mary Madison said suddenly. "Tim is just a year younger than I."

"You're not going to give away all these beautiful Indian things, Doctor?"

The doctor, who had been staring absently into the shadows of the attic, roused herself. "Oh, why not? Merle here isn't the sort that will want to hoard them! I loathe them all. It was just this sort of rubbish—"

She had risen, to fling open the top of one more trunk. Now she moved restlessly across the attic, and Merle, who did not know her mother in this mood, hopped after her.

"It was just this sort of rubbish, little girl," Mary Madison said gently, one of her thin, clever hands laid against the child's cheek, "that made trouble between—your Uncle Timothy and me. Just pictures and rugs—and Aunt Lizzie's will.... Well, let's get through here, and away from these ghosts!"

"I wish *we* had three children," Merle said longingly. "You had your brother. But I haven't any one! Did you hang up your stockings?"

"Dear me, yes! At the dining-room mantel."

"Then I would hang mine there, if I—hanged—it," Merle decided.

"But we have the big open fireplace in the sitting-room now, dear. We didn't have that when we were little, Timmy and I."

"But I'd drather in the dining-room, mother, if that's what you did!"

"Here are perfectly good new flannels—" Miss Frothingham interposed.

"Take them. But Merle," the doctor said, a little troubled, "I would have filled a stocking for you if I had known you really wanted me to, dear. Will you remind me, next Christmas, and I'll see to it?"

"Yes, mother," Merle promised, suddenly lifeless and subdued. "But next Christmas is so—so far," she faltered, with watering eyes and a trembling lip.

"But all the shops are closed now, dear," her mother reminded her sensibly. "You know my brother and I never had a quarrel before," she added, after a space, to the younger woman. "And this was never an open breach."

"Was?" Miss Frothingham echoed, anxious and eager.

"Wasn't. No," said her employer thoughtfully. "It was just a misunderstanding—the wrong word said here, and the wrong construction put upon it there, and then resentment—and silence— our lives separated—"

She fell silent herself, but it was Merle, attentively watching her, who said now:

"Their father's sick, and they aren't going to hang up their stockings!"

"Oh, they've had a great deal of trouble," Miss Frothingham added with a grave expression, as the older woman turned inquiring eyes upon her. "Mr. Rutledge has been ill for weeks and the baby is quite small—six or seven months old, I suppose."

"Why, but he's a successful man!" his sister said impatiently as the other paused.

"Oh yes, they have a good Swedish girl, I know, and a little car, and all that! But I imagine this has been a terribly hard winter for them. They're lovely people, Doctor Madison," added little Miss Frothingham bravely and earnestly. "So wonderful with their

- 132 -

children, and they have a little vegetable garden, and fruit trees, and all that! But all the children in that neighbourhood had whooping-cough last fall, and I know Mrs. Rutledge was pretty tired, and then he got double pneumonia before Thanksgiving, and he hasn't been out of the house since."

"He's a wonderful boy!" Doctor Madison said in a silence. "We were orphans, and he was a wonderful little brother to me. My grandparents were the stern, old-fashioned sort, but Timmy could put fun and life into punishment, even. Many an hour I've spent up here in this very attic with him—in disgrace."

She got up, walked a few paces across the bare floor, picked an old fur buggy-robe from a chair, looked at it absently, and put it down again.

"What insanity brought me up to this attic on a snowy Christmas Eve!" she demanded abruptly, laughing, but with the tears Miss Frothingham had never seen there before in her eyes. "It all comes over me so—what life was when Timmy and George— Merle's father—were in it! Poor little girl," she added, sitting down on a trunk and drawing Merle toward her; "you were to have seven brothers and sisters, and a big daddy to adore you and spoil you! And he had been two months in his grave when she was born," she added to the other woman.

"But then couldn't you afford to have all my brothers and sisters?" Merle demanded anxiously.

"It couldn't be managed, dear. Life gets unmanageable, sometimes," her mother answered, smiling a little sadly. "But a brother is a wonderful thing for a small girl to have. Everything has robbed this child," she added, "the silence between her uncle and me—her father's death—my profession. If I had been merely

- 133 -

a general practitioner, as I was for three years," she went on, "there would have been a score of what we call 'G.P.'s' to fill her poor little stocking! But half my grateful patients hardly know me by sight, much less that I have a greedy little girl who has a stocking to be filled!"

"Mother, I love you," Merle said, for the first time in her life stirred by the unusual hour and mood, and by the tender, half-sorrowful, and all-loving voice she had never heard before.

"And I love you, little girl, even if I am too busy to show it!" her mother answered seriously. "But here! Do let's get done with this before we break our hearts!" she added briskly, in a sudden change of mood. And she sank upon her knees before a trunk and began vigorously to deal with its contents. "And I'll tell you what I'll do, Merle," her mother went on, briskly lifting out and inspecting garments of all sorts. "I'll go to see Mr. Waldteufel on Wednesday—"

"Not Waldteufel of the Bazaar, mother?"

"The very same. You know your daddy and I were boarding with his mother in Potsdam when the war broke out, and two years ago your mother saved his wife and his tiny baby—after two dear little babies had died. So he thinks a great deal of the Madisons, my dear, and he'll give me the very nicest things in that big shop for my little girl's stocking. And suppose you hang it up New Year's Eve this year, and next year—well, we won't say anything about next year now, but just you *wait!*"

"Oh, mother—mother!" Merle sang, her slippered feet dancing. And there was no question at this minute that she would some day be beautiful.

"Don't strangle me. There, I remember that dress—look at the puffed sleeves, Merle," said her mother, still exploring the trunk. "I suppose the velvet is worth something—and the lace collar. That was my best dress."

"Mother, mayn't I keep it? And wear it some day?"

"Why, I suppose you may. I wish," said the doctor in an undertone, whimsically to the other woman, "I wish I had more of that sort of sentiment—of tenderness—in me! I did have, once."

"Perhaps it was the sorrow—and then your taking your profession so hard?" Miss Frothingham suggested timidly.

"Perhaps— Here, this was my brother Timmy's sweater," said the doctor, taking a bulky little garment of grey wool from the trunk. "How proud he was of it! It was his first—'my roll-top sweater,' he used to call it. I remember these two pockets—"

She ran her fingers—the beautifully-tempered fingers of the surgeon—into one of the pockets as she spoke, and Merle and the secretary saw an odd expression come into her face. But when she withdrew her hand and exposed to them the palm, it was filled with nothing more comprehensible than eight or ten curled and crisped old crusts of bread.

"Mother, what is it?" Merle questioned, peering.

"Bait?" Miss Frothingham asked, smiling.

"Crusts," the older woman said in an odd voice.

"Crusts?" echoed the other two, utterly at a loss.

There was that in the doctor's look that made the moment significant.

"Yes," said Merle's mother. And for a full minute there was silence in the attic, Miss Frothingham covertly and somewhat bewilderedly studying her employer's face, Merle looking from one to the other with round eyes like those of a brunette doll, and the older woman staring into space, as if entirely unconscious of their presence.

The lights stirred, and shadows leaped and moved in answer. Snow made a delicate, tinkling sound outside, in the dark, on the roof beyond the dormers. The bell of Saint Paul's rang nine o'clock on Christmas Eve.

"I was always a stubborn child, and I hated the crusts of my bread, but they insisted that I eat them," said Mary Madison suddenly, in an odd, rather low voice. "I used to cry and fight about it, and—and Timmy used to eat them for me."

"Did he like them, mother?" Merle demanded, highly interested.

"Did he—? No, I don't know that he did. But he was a very good little brother to me, Merle. And grandmother and Aunt Lizzie used to be stern with me, always trapping me into trouble, getting me into scenes where I screamed at them and they at me."

Her voice stopped, and for a second she was silent.

"Crusts were a great source of trouble," she resumed after a while.

"I like them!" Merle said encouragingly, to feed the conversation.

"Yours is a very different world, baby. People used to excite and bewilder children thirty years ago. I've spent whole mornings sobbing and defiant. 'You will say it!' 'I won't say it'—hour after hour after hour."

Merle was actually pale at the thought.

"Timmy was the favourite, and how generous he was to me!" his sister said, musing. And suddenly she raised the little dried crusts in both hands to her face, and laid her cheek against them. "Oh, Timmy—Timmy—Timmy!" she said, between a laugh and a sob. "To think of the grimy little hand that put these here just because Molly was so naughty and so stubborn!

"Miss Frothingham," said Doctor Madison quietly, looking up with one of those amazing changes of mood that were the eternal bewilderment of those who dealt with her. "I wonder if you could finish this up? Get Lizzie to help you if you like; we're all but done anyway! Use your own judgment, but when in doubt—destroy! I believe—it's only nine o'clock! I believe I'll go and see my brother! Come. Merle, get your coat with the squirrel collar—it's cold!"

So then it was all Christmas magic, and just what Christmas Eve should be. Saunders brought the little closed car to the door, to be sure, but there he vanished from the scene, and it was only mother and Merle.

The streets were snowy, and snow frosted the wind-shield, and lights and people and the bright windows of shops were all mixed up together, in a pink and blue and gold dazzle of colour.

But all this was past before they came to the "almost country," as Merle called it, and there were gardens and trees about the little houses, where lights streamed out with an infinitely heartening and pleasant effect.

They stopped. "Put your arms tight about my neck, Baby. I can't have you walking in this!" said her mother then.

And Merle tightened her little furry arms about her mother's furry collar, and they somehow struggled and stumbled up to Uncle Tim's porch. There was light in one of the windows, but no light in the hall. But after a while footsteps came.

"Molly!" said the pale, tall, gentle woman who opened the door, "and your dear baby!"

"Cassie—may we come in?" Merle had never heard her mother speak in quite this tone before.

They went in to a sort of red-tinted dimness. But in the

dining-room there was sudden light, and they all blinked at each other. And Merle instantly saw that over the mantel two short stockings and tiny socks were suspended.

The women were talking in short sentences.

"Molly!—"

"Cassie—"

"But in all this snow—"

"We didn't mind it."

"I'm so glad."

"Cassie—how thin you are, child! And you look so tired!"

"Timmy's been so ill!"

"But he's better?"

"Oh yes—but so weak still!"

"You've had a nurse?"

"Not these last two weeks. We couldn't—we didn't—really need her. I have my wonderful Sigma in the kitchen, you know."

"But, my dear, with a tiny baby!"

The worn face brightened. "Ah, he's such a dear! I don't know what we would have done without him!"

A silence. Then Mrs. Rutledge said: "The worst is over, we hope. And the boys have been such a comfort!"

"They hung up their stockings," Merle commented in her deep, serious little voice.

"Yes, dear," their mother said eagerly, as if she were glad to have the little pause bridged. "But I'm afraid Santa Claus is going to be too busy to remember them this year! I've just been telling them that perhaps he wouldn't have time to put anything but some candy and some fruit in this year!"

"*They* believe in Santa Claus," Merle remarked, faintly

reproachful, to her mother. "But I'm younger than Tommy, and I don't!"

"But you may if you want to, dear!" Doctor Madison said, shaken, yet laughing, and kneeling down to put her arms about the little girl. "Cassie, what can I do for Tim?" she pleaded. "We're neither of us children. I don't have to say that I'm sorry—that it's all been a bad dream of coldness and stupidity."

"Oh, Molly—Molly!" the other woman faltered. And tears came into the eyes that had not known them for hard and weary weeks. "He was to blame more than you—I always said so. He knew it! And he did try to write you! He's grieved over it so. But when he met you in the street that day—"

"I know it! I know it! He was wrong—I was wrong—you were the only sensible one, the peacemaker, between us!" the doctor said eagerly and quickly. "It's over. It's for us now to see that the children are wiser in their day and generation!"

"Ah, Molly, but you were always so wonderful!" faltered Cassie Rutledge. And suddenly the two women were in each other's arms. "Molly, we've missed—just *you*—so!" she sobbed.

Two small shabby boys in pyjamas had come solemnly in from the direction of the kitchen, whence also proceeded the fretting of a baby. Merle was introduced to Tommy and Rawley, and was shy. But she immediately took full charge of the baby.

"Santa Claus may not give us anything but apples and stuff," Rawley, who was six, confided. "Because Dad was sick, and there are lots of poor children this year!"

"And we aren't going to have any turkey because Dad and John couldn't have any, anyway!" Tommy added philosophically.

John was the baby, who now looked dewily and sleepily at

the company from above the teething biscuit with which he was smearing his entire countenance.

"He's getting a great, big, hard back tooth, Molly, at eight months," said his mother, casting aside the biscuit and wiping the exquisite, little velvet face. "Isn't that early?"

"It seems so to me. I forget! Any fever?"

"Oh no, but his blessed little mouth is so hot! Timmy's asleep," said Cassie anxiously. "But, Molly, if you could stay to see him just a minute when he wakes! Could Merle—we have an extra bed in the little room right off the boys' room, where the nurse slept. She couldn't spend Christmas with the boys? That would be better than any present to us!"

She spoke as one hardly hoping, and Merle felt no hope whatever. But to the amazement of both, the handsome, resolute face softened, and the doctor merely said:

"Trot along to bed then, Merle, with your cousins. But mind you don't make any noise. Remember, Uncle Timmy is ill!"

Merle strangled her with a kiss. There was a murmur of children's happy voices on the stairs; a messenger came back to ask if Tom's nine-year-old pyjamas or Rawley's seven-year-old size would best suit the guest. Another messenger came discreetly down and hung a fourth stocking at the dining-room mantel, with the air of one both invisible and inaudible.

"He's terrified," said Cassie in an aside, with her good motherly smile; "he knows he has no business downstairs at this hour!"

Then Cassie's baby fretted himself off in her arms, and the two women sat in the dim light, and talked and talked and talked.

"Cassie, we've an enormous turkey—I'll send it over the first thing in the morning."

"But, Molly, when Tim knows you've been here, he'll not care about any turkey!"

"Their stockings—" mused the doctor, unhearing.

With a suddenly lighting face, after deep thought, she went to the telephone in the dining-room, and three minutes later a good husband and father, a mile away across the city, left his own child and the tree he was trimming and went to answer her summons.

"Mr. Waldteufel? This is Doctor Madison."

"Oh, Doctor!" came rushing the rich, European voice. "Merry Christmas to you! I wish could you but zee your bapey—so fat we don't weigh him Sundays no more! His lecks is like—"

The surgeon's voice interrupted. There was excited interchange of words. Then the toy-king said:

"I meet you at my store in ten minutes! It is one more kindness that you ask me to do it! My employees go home at five—the boss he works late, isn't it? I should to work hard for this boy of mine— an egg he eats to-day, the big rough-neck feller!"

"Oh, Molly, you can't!" Cassie protested. But there was colour in her face.

"Oh, Cassie, I can! Have we a tree?"

"I couldn't. It wasn't the money, Molly—don't think that. But it was just being so tired … the trimmings are there from last year … oh, Molly, into this darkness and cold again! You shouldn't!"

She was gone. But the hour that Cassie waited, dreaming, with the baby in her lap, was a restful hour, and when it was ended, and Molly was back again, the baby had to be carried upstairs, up to his crib, for there was heavy work to do below stairs.

Mollie had a coaster and an enormous rocking-horse. She had the car loaded and strapped and covered with packages. She had a tree, which she said she had stolen from the grocer; he would be duly enlightened and paid to-morrow.

She flung off her heavy coat, pinned hack her heavy hair, tied on an apron. She snapped strings, scribbled cards. And she personally stuffed the three larger stockings.

Cassie assisted. Neither woman heard the clock strike eleven.

"You'll be a wreck to-morrow, my dear!"

"Oh, Molly, no! This is just doing me a world of good. I had been feeling so depressed and so worried. But I believe—I do believe—that the worst of it is over now!"

"Which one gets this modelling clay? It's frightfully smelly stuff, but they all adore it! My dear, does Timmy usually sleep this way? I've looked in at him twice, he seems troubled—restless—"

"Yes—the scissors are there, right under your foot. Yes, he is like that, Mollie, no real rest, and he doesn't seem to have any particular life in him. He seems so languid. Nothing tastes exactly right to him and, of course, the children are noisy, and the house is small. I want him—"

Mrs. Rutledge, working away busily in the litter, and fastening a large tinsel ball to a fragrant bough with thin, work-worn hands, stepped back, squinted critically, and turned to the next task. The homely little room was fire-warmed. Mary Madison remembered some of the books, and the big lamp, and the armchair that had belonged to her father. Cassie had a sort of gift for home-making, even in a perfectly commonplace eight-room suburban house, she mused.

"I want him," Cassie resumed presently, "to take us all down south somewhere—or to go by himself, for that matter!—and get a good rest. But he feels it isn't fair to Jim Prescott—his partner, you know. Only—" reasoned the wife, threading glassy little coloured balls with wire, "only Tim is the real brains of the business, and Jim Prescott knows it. Timmy does all the designing, and this year they've seemed to get their first real start—more orders than they can fill, really. And it worries Timmy to fall down just now! He wants to get back. But I feel that if he had a real rest—"

"I don't know," the physician answered, setting John's big brown bear in an attitude of attack above the absurd little sock. "It's a very common attitude, and nine times out of ten a man is happier in his work than idling. I'd let him go back, if I were you, I think."

"Oh, would you, Molly?" Cassie demanded in relief and surprise.

"I think so. And then perhaps you could all get away early to Beachaways—"

"Molly!"

"Don't use that tone, my dear. The place wasn't even opened last year. I went to Canada for some hospital work, and took Merle with me and left her at the Lakes, with my secretary. I wanted then to suggest that you and Timmy use Beachaways. It's in a bad condition, I know—"

"Bad condition! Right there on the beach, and all to ourselves! And he can get away every Friday night!"

"Perhaps you'll have my monkey down with her cousins, now and then. She doesn't seem to have made strangers of them, exactly."

"Not exactly," agreed Cassie with her quiet smile. "They were all crowded into the boys' big bed when I went up. I carried Rawley into the next room. Tom and Merle had their hands clasped, even in their sleep. Molly," she added suddenly in an odd tone, "what—I have to ask you!—what made you come?"

"Christmas, perhaps," the doctor answered gravely, after a moment. "I've always wanted to. But. I'm queer. I couldn't."

"Tim's always wanted to," his wife said. "He's always said: 'There's no real reason for it! But life has just separated us, and we'll have to wait until it all comes straight naturally, again!'"

"I don't think those things ever come straight, naturally," said Mary Madison thoughtfully. "One thinks, 'Well, what's the difference? People aren't necessarily closer, or more congenial, just because they happen to be related!' But at Christmas-time you find it's all true; that families do belong together; that blood is thicker than water!"

"Or when you're in trouble, Molly, or in joy," the other woman said, musing. "Over and over again I've thought that I must go to you—must try to clear up the whole silly business! But you are away so much, and so busy—and so famous now—that somehow I've always hesitated! And just lately, when it seemed"—her voice thickened—"when it seemed as if Timmy really might die," she went on with a little difficulty, "I've felt so much to blame! He's always loved you so, admired you—his big sister! He is always quoting you, what Molly says and does. And just to have the stupid years go on and on, and this silence between us, seemed so—so wasted!"

"Die!" Mollie echoed scornfully. 'Why should he? With these lovely boys and you to live for!"

"Yes, I know. But don't you remember saying years ago, when you were just beginning to study medicine to have an intelligent interest in George's work—don't you remember saying then that dying is a point of view? That you had seen a sudden sort of meekness come over persons who really weren't very sick, just as if they thought to themselves: 'What now? Oh yes. I'm to die?' I remember our all shouting when you said it, but many a time since I've thought it was true. And somehow it's been almost that way with Timmy, lately. Just—dying because he was through—living!"

"Cassie, what utter foolishness to talk that way, and get yourself crying when you are tired out, anyway!"

"Ah well, I believe just the sight of you when he wakes up is going to cure him, Molly!" his wife smiled through her tears.

But only a little later the invalid fell, as it chanced, into the most restful sleep he had known for weeks, and Mary, creeping away to her car, under the cold, high moon, and hearing the Christmas bells ring midnight as she went over the muffling snow toward her own room and her own bed, could only promise that when she had had a bath, and some sleep, she would come back and perhaps be beside him when he awakened.

And so it happened that in the late dawn, when three little wrappered forms were stirring in the Rutledge nursery, and when thrilled whispers were sounding in the halls, Merle Madison was amazed to see her mother coming quietly up from the kitchen and could give her an ecstatic Christmas kiss.

"We know it's only oranges and candy," breathed Merle, "but we're going down to get our stockings now!"

"Is the tree lighted?" Mary Madison, who was carrying a steaming bowl, asked in French.

"It is simply a vision!" the other mother, whose pale face was radiant, answered, with her lips close to the curly head of the excited baby she was carrying. "Timmy's waking," she added, with a nod toward the bedroom door.

"I'll go in."

The other woman carried her burden across the threshold—in the quiet, orderly sick-room her eyes and her brother's eyes met for the first time in years.

He was very white and thin, unshorn, and somehow he reminded her of the unkempt little motherless boy of years ago.

"Molly!" he whispered, his lips trembling.

And her own mouth shook as she put the howl on the bedside table, and sat down beside him, and clasped her fine, strong, warm hand over his thin one.

"Hello, Timmy," she said gently, blinking and with a little thickness of speech.

"Molly," he whispered again in infinite content. And she felt his fingers tighten, and saw two tears slip through the closed eyelids as his head was laid back against the pillow.

"Weak," he murmured, without stirring.

"You've been so sick, dear."

A silence. Then he said. "Molly, were you here in the night?"

"Just to peep at you, Timmy!"

"I thought you were. It was so delicious even to dream it. I didn't dare ask Cassie, for fear it was only a dream. Cassie's been an angel, Molly!"

"She always was, Tim. You and I were the demon liars."

"'Demon liars'! Oh, do you remember the whipping we got for yelling that at each other?"

"Do you remember that we agreed that 'yellow cats' would mean all the very worst and naughtiest things that ever were, and the grown-ups would never know what it meant?"

"Don't I!"

He submitted childishly to her ministrations. She washed his face, brushed his hair, settled herself beside him with the steaming bowl.

"Come now, Timmy. Christmas breakfast!"

"Do you remember crying for mother, that first Christmas in the old house?"

"Ah, my dear! Fancy what she must have felt to leave us!"

"I've thought of that so often, since the boys have grown big enough to love us, and want to be with us!"

"My girl is with them downstairs—I'll have to tell you what a Christmas we've made for them! The place looks like a toy-shop! Timmy, I hope they'll always like her, be to her like the own brothers that she never had!" So much Mary said aloud. But to herself she was saying: "He doesn't seem to know it, but that's fully two ounces—three ounces—of good hot bread and milk he's taken. Well, was it a riot?" she added to Cassie, who came quietly in to sit on the foot of the bed and study the invalid with loving and anxiously smiling eyes.

"Mary, you should have seen it! It was too wonderful," said Cassie, who had been crying. "I never saw anything like the expression on their little faces when I opened the door. Merle was absolutely white—Tom gave one yell! It was a sight—the candles all lighted, the floor heaped, the mantel loaded. I suppose there never was such a Christmas!

"Cassie, you wouldn't taste this? It is the most delicious milk-toast I ever tasted in my life!" Tim said.

"If it tastes good to you. dearest!"

"I don't know how Molly makes it. Molly, do you suppose you could show Sigma how you do it?"

– 147 –

"I think so, Tim." The women exchanged level quick glances of perfect comprehension, and there was heaven in their eyes.

"There isn't any more downstairs?"

"I don't know that I would now, Timmy," dictatorial and imperious Doctor Madison said mildly. "You can have more when I get back from the hospital, say at about one. Now you have to sleep—lots, all the time, for days! I'm going to take all the children to my house for dinner and overnight. You're not to hear a sound. Look at the bowl, Cassie!"

She triumphantly inverted it. It was clean.

"Do you remember," Mary Madison asked, holding her brother's hands again, "do you remember, years ago, when you used to eat my crusts for me, Timmy?"

"And is this bread upon the water, Molly?" he asked, infinitely satisfied to lie smiling at the two women who loved him. "I ate your crusts, and now you come and turn other crusts into milk-toast for me!"

"But don't you remember?"

He faintly shook his head. It was long ago forgotten, the little-boy kindness and loyalty, in the days of warts and freckles, cinnamon sticks and skate-keys, tears that were smeared into dirty faces; long, incomprehensibly boring days in chalk and ink-scented schoolrooms; long, blissful vacation forenoons dreaming under bridges, idling in the sweet dimness of old barns. There had been a little passionate Molly, alternately satisfactory and naughty, tearing aprons and planning Indian encampments, generous with cookies and taffies, exacting and jealous, marvellous, maddening, and always to be protected and admired. But she was a dim, hazy long-ago memory, merged now into the handsome, brilliant woman whose fine hand held his.

"He used to fill his little pockets with them, Cassie. I can remember passing them to him, under the table."

"Our Tim is like that," Cassie nodded.

"Think of your remembering," Tim murmured contentedly.

He did not, but then it did not matter. It was Christmas morning, the restless, dark night was over. Sun was shining outdoors on the new snow. His adored boys were happy, and the baby was asleep, and Cassie, instead of showing the long strain and anxiety, looked absolutely blooming as she smiled at him. Best of all, here was Molly, back in his life again, and talking of teaching the boys swimming, down at beloved old Beachaways. He had always thought, when he was a little boy, that no felicity in heaven or earth equalled a supper on the shore at Beachaways. The grown-ups of those days must have been hard, indeed, thought Tim mildly, drifting off to sleep, for he could remember begging for the joy of taking sandwiches down there, and being coldly, and unreasonably—he could see now—refused. Well, it would be different with his kids. They could be pirates, smugglers, beach-combers, whale-fishers, anything they pleased. They could build driftwood fires and cook potatoes and toast bread.

"Crusts, hey?" he said drowsily. "Bread upon the waters."

"Bread is oddly symbolical anyway, isn't it, Molly?" Cassie said, in her quiet, restful voice. "Bread upon the waters, and the breaking of bread, and giving the children stones when they ask for bread! Even the solemnest words of all—'Do this in commemoration'—are of bread."

"Perhaps there is something we don't understand about it," Molly answered very softly. "The real sacrament of love—the essence of all religion and all sacraments."

She thought of the little crusts still in the pocket of the roll-top sweater, she looked at the empty bowl, and she held Tim's thin hand warmly, steadily.

"Christmas bread," she said, as if to herself.

Christmas in a Bavarian Village

ELIZABETH VON ARNIM

When I got out of the train in the dusk of a dove-coloured afternoon, my daughter ran along the platform to meet me, and with her ran a young man in short leather breeches with bare knees, and it being almost dark, and the costume familiar, I thought it was her husband. So that I greeted him with the proper enthusiasm, seizing his hands in both mine, and crying, "How charming of you to come out in all the cold!"

Fortunately my son-in-law and I do not kiss, but except for that all was enthusiasm, including, or course, the familiar *Du*.

My daughter pulled my arm. "It's the taxi-man," she whispered, struggling to suppress her giggles.

The young man, I must say, let my behaviour wash over him with dignity. Perhaps he thought it was the way all foreigners arrived at stations, and that, far from being a cold race, the English were red hot.

A little subdued, I was led out of the station into a world of Christmas trees. In front of most of the houses stood a tree lit by electric light, and in the middle of the one wide street was a huge one, a pyramid of solemn radiance.

I felt as if I had walked into a Christmas card—glittering snow, steep-roofed old houses, and the complete windlessness, too, of a Christmas card. Not since 1909 had I had a German Christmas, the last of a string of them, and seeing that 1909 is a long while ago, and that many things have happened since, it was odd how much at home I felt, how familiar everything seemed, and how easily this might have been the Christmas, following in its due order, of 1910.

On the doorstep of the little house in the middle of snowfields and ringed round with towering mountains, stood, full welcome, my real son-in-law. He was dressed exactly like the taxi-man, in leather shorts and an embroidered shirt, so how could anybody be expected to know which was which? Carefully I looked at him, though embarking, this time, on warmth. "How charming of you," I cried, when thoroughly certain, "to come out in all the cold!"—for I have not many German sentences and the same has to do several times.

Not only was he on the doorstep, but many enchanting smells, very beautiful to the hungry, were there, too, smells of *Leberkuchen*, *Leberwurst*, red cabbage, roasting goose, and the more serious smell, serious because it also attends funerals and envelops mausoleums, of the fir tree standing ready to be lit in the drawing room.

This was Christmas Eve, the day the Germans, in the evening, celebrate; and while I was taking off my things upstairs, the candles on the tree were lit, so that when I came down the household, consisting of father, mother, small daughter, three white-capped and white-cotton-gloved maids, and two Scotties, were waiting for me in the hall before the shut door of the room of mysteries.

To the strains of *Stille Nacht, heilige Nacht*, we marched in according to age, beginning with the youngest and ending, after me, with the cook. Since, for sometime past, everybody seems to be younger than I am, I was quite pleased about the cook.

I knew exactly what I would find inside the room, for had I not for years myself arranged such rooms with their tree and tables of presents? There were the tables in a familiar row, one for each person, piled with parcels tied up in gay paper and silver ribbon, decorated with pots of cyclamen and azaleas, and there was the tree, with the little crèche at its feet, and marzipan sheep flocking round chocolate Wise Men.

We stood in a semicircle, keeping our eyes fixed on the tree and not letting them wander to the tables, because that wouldn't have been manners, and while we were busy singing *Stille Nacht* to the accompanying gramophone, the Scotties, who had no manners, before our outraged eyes ate, one after the other, all the marzipan sheep. Because of custom we couldn't do anything but stand stiff and sing. Both tradition and decency rooted us in immobility. Luckily there were only two verses, and the Wise Men were saved in the nick of time and I thought only Germans could be as disciplined as that, and able by training to appear absorbed in holy words while their hearts must be boiling within them.

But the conduct of the Scotties delayed us in getting to our tables. They had to be dealt with and banished before we were able to turn our attention to joy. Those dogs didn't care a bit that they were disgraced. Inside them, safely tucked away, were the sheep, and I could have sworn they laughed as they were led away.

Slightly subdued—this was the second time I had been subdued—for it seemed a sad thing for the family to lose so many sheep, bought, I knew, this Christmas all fresh and new for me, and destined to appear at least at five Christmases more, I began undoing my parcels, and soon we all got worked up to the proper spirit again. From each table came cries of excitement and joy. From each table somebody was rushing continually to thank and hug, or thank and kiss the hand of somebody else. Even the cook and myself, the *doyennes* of the party, were ready to hug. She luckily, had soon to withdraw to the kitchen, to give the finishing touches to the goose, or I don't know but what we too mightn't have ended in each other's arms.

Wading through torn paper and silver ribbon we went in to dinner, drank, made speeches, and were merry. After dinner we waded back, again, and were less merry and after we had eaten *Baumkuchen* and drunk hot spiced wine we were hardly merry at all, because we would have liked, but couldn't because of tradition and decency, to go to sleep.

"It's impossible," I said, shaking myself free of the stupor slowly bearing me down, "to imagine this Germany is any different from the Germany I knew."

"Oh, but it is—" began my daughter, instantly to be stopped by her husband with a quick, "Take care—", for one of the maids had come into the room.

This woke me up completely. Take care? What of?

Slightly subdued, for the third time, I allowed myself to be put into my fur coat, and driven to midnight mass. A glittering night. A night of peace and beauty. The bells of the old church on the hill were ringing, and streams of dark figures—*streams*, I noted with astonishment—piously silent, were flowing up towards it. Down in the street the huge Christmas tree stood radiant. On each grave in the churchyard a tiny one burnt, lighting up the whole place with symbols of remembrance and love. And inside the church, packed so tightly together that we could hardly get through, was a crowd so devout, so intent on worship, and absorbed in the beauty of the singing (once more) of *Stille Nact*, that I, who read my *Times* and know what is happening to the churches of Germany, couldn't believe my eyes.

"But—" I began, as I hung on to my son-in-law's arm.

"Take care," he quickly whispered gripping my hand.

Take care. Again. Must one then for ever take so much care? And, after all, what had I said except "But"?

Freedom

NANCY MORRISON

❄

Sylvia Grey, late for dinner as usual, came running down the wide, thickly-carpeted staircase, and stopped at the desk of the *concierge*, her grey eyes anxious. Has that letter I'm expecting come yet?"

The genial Swiss glanced at the pigeon-hole above him and shook his bald head, smiling at her in frank admiration of a pretty woman.

"I am sorry to disappoint you again, *madame*. To-morrow by the first post, perhaps, it shall come."

A blank expression supplanted the eagerness on her small, pointed face, and she stood for a moment as though she could scarcely believe what he told her. Then, with an odd little smile of resignation, she nodded and hurried into the dining-room.

The *concierge*, watching the graceful, flying figure, was moved to wonder. Why should she be so anxious for a letter, this thin little English miss with the *cendre* hair? Money was certainly not the cause of her worry—the wad of banknotes she had left in his care could testify to that. As for a lover—well, surely one love affair at a time was enough for anyone; that she and the tall English doctor were mutually attracted was patent even to such dull wits as that fool of a hall-porter and the manager's ugly typist.

Then he shrugged his shoulders. Perhaps it was from a woman she expected the letter, not a man. Women wrote to each other sometimes, after all. A relative might be sick—a mother or a sister. And he dismissed the subject of the pretty English girl's anxieties from his mind in favour of the more mundane matter of a pair of skis reported missing from the sports shed.

Sylvia, slipping into her usual place at the big centre table beside John Paton, tried, too, to forget the missing letter. Tried to lose herself, as she had so often done, even against her will, in the intoxication of John's nearness—in the thrill of his voice, lowered to murmur some trifling remark meant only for her to hear—in the heady joy of that look in his keen blue eyes.

But to-night worry sat too heavy on her shoulders, and when he teased her for her slackness in not entering for the novices' race that afternoon, she found it difficult, for once, to respond.

When was the letter coming that should give her the freedom she had learned these last three weeks to crave? When would Mark write to break the chain which bound her fast to him?

That he would refuse to set her free was unthinkable. Angry as he would be at her running off to Switzerland like this, surely he would be open to reason. She had told him frankly of her love for John Paton—a love which had come to her against her will—a love which,' if she denied it and trampled it underfoot, would never flower in her life again. Surely this cry from her heart would pierce his armour of hardness and cynicism. Surely, surely, he would consent to set her free!

She made a gallant attempt to eat, joining in the laughter of the light-hearted folk about her, who taxed her with "banting" for the fashionable ski-suit figure, but was glad to accept John's offer of a little champagne to "buck her up." He was a dear, was John. He always seemed to understand when one was tired and only pretending to be gay.

But before the champagne arrived the head waiter came bustling up with a message.

"A telephone call for you from Paris, *madame*."

She rose quickly to her feet, her face whitening. She had never for one moment anticipated that Mark would communicate with her by telephone. And from Paris! What did it mean? Was it a good or a bad omen?

The short walk along the hall to the manager's office seemed endless. But at last she was sitting down at the desk, speaking into the 'phone.

Mark's voice, clear and crisp, cut brusquely across her opening words of greeting.

"Oh, spare me all that, Sylvia! What on earth are you up to at Wengen? I thought you had gone to the Riviera, from what you said in the note you left for me."

"I meant to. But in Paris I saw a poster of the snow and the mountains. So I came on here instead."

A sound that resembled a snort came over the line.

"Well, I hope to goodness you're taking care of yourself, and not playing the fool, Sylvia. I don't mind your skating, but—"

"Oh, I'm taking care all right. But, Mark, what are you doing in Paris? And didn't you get my letter?, I wrote nearly five days ago."

"Letter? Of course I did. But I hope you didn't imagine I should take it seriously. A lot of moonshine! Anyway, I tell you here and now that I refuse absolutely to free you, and that I'm on my way now to fetch you back to London. I leave Paris to-night and I arrive at Wengen about mid-day to-morrow."

"It's no good your doing that, Mark," Sylvia exclaimed passionately. "I tell you that I'm in love with this man—in love for the first time in my life. I know he's going to ask me soon to marry him—perhaps to-night. And when he does, I'm going to say 'Yes,' and go back to East Africa with him. I've never had any real happiness all my life, and now the chance has come to taste it I'm not going to let it slip away."

"Happiness! My dear Sylvia, don't for goodness' sake start getting sentimental." Sylvia could almost see him shifting his cigar from one side of his mouth to the other. "You've got most of the things that other women would sell their souls for. Youth, good looks, wealth and health, to say nothing of—"

"I haven't ever had love," Sylvia said with a kind of despairing intensity. "No one is going to do me out of that—not even you, Mark."

"Oh, don't talk rot, my dear!" Mark's voice was impatient. "If I did set you free to do as you liked, you'd soon be jolly sorry. Life as a poor man's wife in Kenya wouldn't suit you long. But anyway, the question doesn't arise, because I absolutely refuse to do what you ask. Good-bye till to-morrow. And, for the love of Mike, take care of yourself!"

She heard the click that told her he had rung off, and hung up the receiver. Then sitting back in the chair she covered her face in her hands, while all the dream castles she had fashioned these last three weeks came tumbling in ruins about her ears.

Life was too cruel. If she had guessed for one moment that she would ever fall in love like this, she would never have tied herself to Mark; however firmly he had set that iron will of his against hers.

She heard the manager's discreet cough at the door, and with an effort pulled herself together. She mustn't give way like this and have everyone staring at her and asking if she had had bad news. She mustn't, whatever happened, give John a chance to speak. She was bound, as surely as though she had iron manacles round her wrists. But John must never gain the fruitless knowledge that she was chained, and for his sake was breaking her heart to be free.

She went back to the dining-room, a smile on her lips, and forced herself into a sparkling gaiety that spread round the table like a flame. Champagne and more champagne was brought, and the noise and laughter rose to a higher key.

Only John Paton did not join in the merriment. He had never seen Sylvia in this mood, and it troubled him. Besides, she was drinking more than was good for her. Even if he hadn't loved her, a girl like that, here alone, with no one to look after her ...

He bent down to whisper, and at the sound of his voice Sylvia's hand shook, so that the golden wine brimmed over her glass.

"Come along out of the noise and heat, Sylvia. Get your snow-shoes and leather coat on, and I'll take you out on the *luge* run."

She shook her head, laughing, and answered him more loudly than was necessary.

"No thanks, John. Not in this." And glanced down at her short, silver dress.

"Oh, I won't spill you over. You needn't be nervous."

Her laughter took a scoffing note.

"Nervous! Why do you always harp on my nervousness? Anyone would think I was a perfect booby—an absolute little funk-stick."

"Well, Miss Grey, so far as ski-ing is concerned, you don't show any keen desire to get off the practice slopes and come higher up." The tall, dark girl opposite her smiled a shade too pleasantly. "You can't really blame Dr. Paton for supposing you to be nervous."

Sylvia flushed at the studied insult. But it was her own fault. She shouldn't have laid herself open to it, when there was no chance of explaining.

But a sudden resolution crystallised in her brain. There was a way out—one way only—by which she could hope to gain her freedom. Why hadn't she thought of it before?

She stood up and held her glass aloft.

"Nervous or not, I'm coming out on the run to-morrow. Who'll drink to my first expedition?"

Amid fresh laughter and noise the toast was drunk. But John's face, as he sat down again, was grave and troubled.

"I don't think you ought to come to-morrow, Sylvia," he said, under his breath. "We shall be coming down from Wengern-Alp the difficult way, round Hell Corner and over the bumps. Even if I brought you by the easier way, there's a wood path to tackle that's like ice just now."

She fidgetted with a fork.

"John, you're absurd. Lots of beginners come down from Wengern-Alp."

"I know. But not when there's so little depth of snow. Falling is no joke just at present. Why don't you wait for a day or two? We're sure to have a fresh fall of snow by then."

Sylvia flung back her small blonde head and jumped once more to her feet.

"I'm coming to-morrow," she said. "And meanwhile there's the band striking up. On with the dance!"

As the evening went by, the reckless gaiety of her mood increased, and not one bar did she miss of any dance.

Usually, in spite of a besieging crowd—for she was by far the best dancer in the hotel—she gave most of her dances to John. But to-night she was ready to dance with all and sundry, and presently John, bewildered and hurt by her casual manner, left the ballroom and went to bed.

He lay awake for an hour or two, trying to arrive at a reasonable explanation of Sylvia's mood, which was obviously engendered by her 'phone call from Paris; and then, unable to solve the problem, very sensibly went to sleep, determined to "have it out" with the girl the next day.

But to Sylvia, when at last she went up to her room, sleep refused to come. And it was not until dawn silvered the sky that she sank into a deep and dreamless slumber.

When she awoke the room was flooded with sunlight. She looked at her watch, found that it was nine o'clock, and rang for her breakfast. If she were to catch the ten-ten train with the others to go up the mountains, she would have to hurry. There would be no time for more than a splash in the bathroom. Ski-ing attire couldn't be put on in a couple of ticks, like day clothes; and those ankle puttees always took ages.

There was a chorus of surprise when, just before ten, she came down, neat and workmanlike in her dark blue suit, and joined the waiting group in the hall.

"Miss Grey, you're not really coming?"

"But, my dear, you'll find it awfully stiff for your first run. And the snow's like ice."

"Really, you oughtn't to try the bumps till you've had more practice."

She waved all their protests aside. She was as strong as a horse, and not a scrap nervous. If they were afraid she would hold them back, they needn't worry. She felt she could tackle anything.

While they were still chattering and arguing John came striding along the hall, and stopped short at the sight of her.

"Sylvia, you're not really coming?"

She smiled equably.

"But of course. It's high time, as you've often said, that I got away from the nursery slopes and came out for a proper run."

He shrugged his shoulders.

"Very well. But it's rather a reckless sort of thing to do."

She smiled again.

"I feel reckless," she said.

❄

The half-dozen or so who undertook that run from Scheidegg to Wengern-Alp and round Hell Corner that day never forgot it. Never forgot the way Sylvia Grey, seemingly unconscious of danger and devoid of fear, pressed on behind John Paton, following without hesitation where he led, tumbling more often than any of the others, but always up again on the instant and thrusting forward again. They had never, they said, seen a beginner with nerve like that. ...

And truth to tell, there was no fear in her. Nothing but dark despair, lightened by one tiny gleam of hope—the hope that sprang from that deep resolve of the night before.

Before they came to the steep, hilly fields, known by the nickname of "the bumps," John gave her a word of warning.

"You've been doing splendidly. But I want you to follow the other two women now. I always take the bumps straight, and go over them hell-for-leather. But you must tack, like the others. Even then you won't find it easy. Crouch as low as you can and keep your knees bent. I'll wait for you at the top of the wood."

He started off, his figure poised like that of a young god, and after a second's sickening hesitation, Sylvia followed him. She heard shouts behind her.

"Miss Grey—you can't take them straight! Tack, for goodness' sake!" But she took no notice. Her teeth set, her figure crouched low down on the skis, she followed that skimming, dipping form in front.

On and on—down, down, and then swiftly up again; there was no stopping now. The pace was terrible, over that icy surface, and the wind whisked off her beret and whistled through her hair.

On and on, till she was conscious now of nothing but the deadening fear of the fall which she knew must inevitably come. And, at last, on a sharp uprise, the mad flight ceased abruptly, and she was flung violently into the air and then down again on her side.

For what seemed an eternity she lay still in the white silence, suffering intense pain. And then there were people round her, taking her skis off and making them into a litter to carry her back up the snowy slope to the railway line. Presently there was John, too, dripping with sweat from his swift climb back over the bumps—John bandaging her injured knee—John trying not to hurt her.

When he had finished, he bent over her.

"I'm not going to lecture you now," he whispered. "But, Sylvia, you brave little fool, I love you!"

She smiled up at him, tried to say something, but went off, instead, into a merciful faint.

At last the little procession reached the hotel. There was the usual bustle and excitement attendant on an accident, but promptly, under John's supervision, Sylvia, who was conscious again now, but in great pain, was given an opiate and put to bed.

And then the manager came hurrying up to him.

"There's a gentleman arrived a short time ago from Paris, sir. He's come to see Miss Grey. He told me that he would be staying the night and that he and Miss Grey would be leaving in the morning."

For a moment John's heart seemed to stop beating.

"You want me to see him on Miss Grey's behalf?"

The man made a deprecating gesture.

"If you please, sir. It would be better perhaps if you would explain about the accident."

John nodded, and followed the manager into a small private sitting-room. And the next minute was facing a scowling stranger whose features, cast in Southern mould, were oddly familiar to him.

"Where's Miss Grey?" the stranger barked. "Why doesn't she come herself, instead of sending you?"

With a mighty effort Paton checked his anger.

"I'm a doctor," he explained stiffly. "Miss Grey has had an accident. She hurt her knee this afternoon, ski-ing."

The man's face took on an almost livid tint.

"Then she's done it on purpose! I told her last night over the telephone that I wouldn't let her break her contract with me. And so she's planned this accident. It's genuine, I suppose?"

"Perfectly genuine," Paton said coldly. "But I am afraid I don't quite understand. What contract are you referring to?"

The stranger's anger gave place for a moment to sheer astonishment.

"What sort of a contract do you suppose Sylvia Grey would have?" he demanded, and produced a card. "Do you mean to tell me you've never heard of Sylvia Grey, the dancer—nor of me?"

Mechanically John took the card and read the name:

MR. MARK GREENFIELD.

"Of course," he said, half stupidly. "I've seen several of your productions. Not lately, though."

"I imagine not. Otherwise you would have recognised Sylvia."

"I don't know." John's voice was weary. "None of the other people here seem to have spotted her. Sylvia Grey is a pretty common name. And she doesn't look like a revue star, does she?"

Greenfield's answer was a grunt.

"I suppose she thinks she's fooled me and got out of her contract."

"But I don't understand," John repeated. "Why should she take such extreme measures to break her contract?"

"Because the little fool thinks she's fallen in love," Greenfield retorted contemptuously. "There's some man here she's gone dippy over and wants to marry. She was going on about him over the 'phone last night as though she were a schoolgirl."

He took out a cigar and lit it.

"But they're all alike, these actresses. Ungrateful, featherheaded little hussies!" Then as if suddenly thinking of it, he handed his cigar-case to John. "I'd like to see her at the very first opportunity," he went on, ignoring John's refusal. "It would give me supreme pleasure to tell her what I think of her."

"You can't see her this evening," John said, tightening his lips. "She's under an opiate. I had to give it to her because she was suffering such pain."

"I'm sorry for that part of it," Greenfield said gruffly. "But it's her own fault. Even if the accident wasn't deliberately planned, she knows she has no earthly right to take part in these dam-fool sports. You'd better wire to Berne for the best specialist you can get hold of. Money's no object. My new show's due to start in less than a month, and every day she's out of it means a loss to me in hard cash."

John looked at him squarely.

"Whatever is done or isn't done, Mr. Greenfield," he said,"" Miss Grey will not be able to dance for the next six months."

❄

Coming to, in the darkened bedroom, Sylvia opened her eyes and saw John Paton sitting motionless in an armchair.

She called to him, and he came and bent over her.

"John," she said painfully, "has—has Mark come? Does he know about my knee?"

John nodded; then stooped lower.

"Sylvia, is it true what he said? That you planned this accident so that you could get out of your contract?"

The shadow of a smile flickered across her pale face.

"It's almost true. Only at the end it really was an accident. It wasn't necessary to engineer one." Then her lids began to flutter and she plucked with nervous fingers at the counterpane. "John, do you think it was dreadful of me? It was an iniquitous contract Mark made me sign—everyone said so afterwards, when it was too late. It tied me to him for years and years. Of course when I signed it I thought I was very lucky—I didn't realise, as Mark did, that I had the makings of a star. Nor that—"

She broke off. John's lips were so close to her now that they almost brushed her forehead.

"And was that other thing he said true?" he demanded gently. "That the reason you wanted to break your contract was that you had met some man here you loved and wanted to be free to marry?"

She did not speak, nor move her head. But her eyes told him all he wanted to know.

He bent the fraction of an inch lower. And his lips, from touching her hair, sought her mouth.

On Skating

CORNELIA OTIS SKINNER

It is my cross in life to be completely unathletic. At college I was a member of the seventh hockey I team. Hockey was compulsory; there were only seven teams and the seventh rarely met, because there was no one bad enough to meet them. The instructor who taught us fencing, after the first lesson, advised me to take up folk dancing, and the night after I got over the horse in gym, my class gave me a dinner. True, at school I was at the head of an awkward squad that had to do deep-breathing exercises during the recess period, but after a month a new athletic teacher decided we weren't worth the trouble and turned us into a raw egg and Sanatogen list. Since that remote time, no poet has ever sought the inspired word more avidly than I the form of exercise I can pursue without looking like one of the Fratellini brothers. I ought to realize that it is a fruitless quest, and stick to yeast and vibrating machines; but now and again the urge re-awakens and I embrace some new sport with desperate ambition, only to sink into a neurasthenia of wondering if perhaps I'm not suffering from rickets. However, there seems to be nothing wrong with me physically. My heart is the kind doctors call in other doctors to listen to; my blood pressure is doing whatever a blood pressure should, and, unless I attempt some set form of exercise, I apparently co-ordinate."

Elise listened to me with compassion. She too suffered from having a spirit of the White Maid of Astolat imprisoned in the body of a great bouncing outdoor girl. Moreover, as she had been eating too well, she was losing the bouncing quality and felt that something should be done about it. The previous winter she had taken up golf at Wanamaker's and I had turned my hand (or rather my ankle) at soft shoe dancing. But Elise found that the subway gave her sinus trouble and my instructor told me that if only I'd started younger he'd have been able to "place" me in burlesque; so we again found ourselves thrown on a sporting world without a muscle between us.

It was a cold day and we were walking in the Park. The long clean hiss of skates cutting new ice rose from the pond. It sounded fresh and wholesome above the roar and rumble of the Great City, as a milk churn would sound in a cocktail bar. A handful of people was gliding about the white surface below us in delicious cadence.

"Do you know how to skate?" asked Elise.

"Do you know how to walk a tight rope?" I replied. We admitted we neither of us knew how to do either but would like to learn and of the two pastimes skating seemed the more practical.

"It seems a lot to learn for so short a season," I ventured.

"But think what a help it would be at St. Moritz."

The fact that neither Elise nor I can go abroad except in the middle of summer did not in the least dim our ardor.

"We might come here tomorrow," I suggested.

"We'll have to take some indoor lessons first." Elise appeared to know all about it.

'Where? At Ned Wayburn's?"

"No. One goes to a sort of academy and hires an instructor." And we arranged to meet next day at the Palais de Glace or whatever our city's glorified ice-house calls itself.

After twenty-four hours I must admit the nap had a bit worn off (if there is a nap on ice). The marble approach to the skating edifice with its uniformed guard and gold paneled walls had more of a Roxy than a Hans Brinker atmosphere. I advanced to the "guichet" and found myself asking for a seat on the parterre (a location, I ruefully reflected, in which I was only too likely and too frequently to be). Someone handed me a pink ticket and timidly I entered the chilly building.

An orchestra was playing the "Blue Danube," apparently assuming that stately river froze over every winter, and to its measure some two dozen couples were twirling swiftly and gracefully about a vast arena. Silent pairs glided around the outer edge, a wild youth was racing past them as if he'd been carrying the good news from Ghent to Aix and had lost the way, and in the center a little group of serious skaters were studying the intricacies of the figure eight, seemingly mistaking it for the Einstein theory. My heart was pounding with what I told myself was delight. "What a sport! What a sport!" I thought (or tried to), breathing deep of the ammonia-scented air and endeavoring to hear the music above the sudden roar of an elevated train. I was standing near the instructors. I knew they were instructors because their caps said so. Stalwart fellows they were, clad in uniforms of Lincoln green. They looked like Robin Hood's Merrie Men, except that they weren't especially merrie.

Elise arrived. She was going to a wedding later and was wearing a chiffon-velvet dress, a broadtail coat and white kid gloves. I asked her if she wasn't a little overdressed, but she said she thought not, and, as a concession to sport, changed the white kid gloves for a pair of gray mittens. We stood for a time uncertain what to do, until the kindly soul who kept the appointment book told us the young lady in the dressing room would fit us to skates. A shudder went through me as if she had said thumbscrews.

The young lady in the dressing room was colored and bored with life. Our entrance was an interruption to her perusal of a tabloid. She asked us resentfully what size skates we wore. (She might as well have asked what size diving bell I required.) After glancing scornfully at my foot she called to a hidden confederate, "Marie! Send up a large pair!" Marie told her to come and get them, and she shambled away leaving me feeling like someone who, trying to purchase a dress in the misses' department, is told she will find what she wants at Lane Bryant. After a bit she impassively returned with two objects of torture—high laced shoes that I suspected had been left there by a Boston welfare worker, and fastened to their soles a glittering example of the steel-forger's art that weighed incredibly. After thrusting my feet into the boots she laced them so tightly I was about to scream when she took a buttonhook from her belt and pulled the laces until she'd made an excellent tourniquet at each ankle.

"Aren't you stopping the circulation?" I suggested.

"I guess so," she replied and I thought what a pity I hadn't been bitten by a rattlesnake. "You don't feel the cold, see," she explained. She was right. After ten minutes I didn't feel anything.

The operation was repeated on Elise, who bore it bravely; after which the young lady returned to her tabloid and left us sitting helplessly on the bench.

"How do your new shoes hurt?" croaked Elise

"Very well, thank you," I replied. "I suppose we'd better go on in."

"How?" asked Elise. "Do we coast down this wooden passageway?"

"No. We walk, of course."

"Don't be funny. Someone will have to carry me "

"You don't expect to be carried about the ice, do you?" I retorted. "Come on, Elise, it isn't far." And I sprang courageously to my feet, which turned out not to be where they usually were—a surprise that precipitated me back onto the bench.

"A well-equipped place like this ought to have wheel chairs," I said savagely.

"Hold the wall," came the tired voice of the young lady.

"How can you hold a wall!" snarled Elise. She had risen and was swaying like a helmsman in a gale.

"If worse comes to worst we can always crawl," I said and wondered what one did in case of fire.

Lurching, clutching at benches and one another, we managed to progress down the passageway with the grace of trained bears and emerge near the group of instructors in Lincoln green. The appointment-book lady called out that someone named Kelly was to take Elise, and I saw her go away pale but gallant. There was some muttered conversation among the Merrie Men as to who was to take me. The chosen instructor apparently didn't feel adequate. At length, a great creature, the Little John of the band, loomed up to me and said "I'll take you, lady," as Hercules might have said, "Allow me, Atlas."

"I hate to bother you," I murmured.

"It's a pleasure," replied my gallant and steered me toward the ice. Here he paused, crossed my arms and, after doing the same with his own, seized my hands in a vice-like grip. I wondered if he wanted to play "Wringing the dish-rag," but with a swift spring he sailed onto the ice and yanked me after him irretrievably into the frozen waste. For a few moment things looked very bad indeed and the instructor and I looked even worse. We bent violently to one side, then to the other, then bowed forward several times like Moslems salaaming Mecca. Now I was ahead of my partner, now behind him; the next second found me wrapped about him like a drunkard about a lamp-post. He meantime was maintaining his equilibrium and murmuring "Steady! Steady!" as if he thought I was Twenty Grand. At moments we were arm's length apart, only to come together in a passionate embrace that made mc feel he ought to ask me to marry him. My ankles, meantime, were giving me all the support of india rubber. They bent and turned as I never knew they could and most of the time I was progressing on the side of my shoe.

"How is it you ain't never skated when you was a kid?" my Merrie Man panted. We had traversed the length of the room and were pausing for breath. For lack of a better excuse I said I had always lived in Cuba and wondered what I'd do if he started speaking to me in Spanish.

"Couldn't you let yourself go more?" he asked.

"Go where?" I inquired, but he didn't seem to know. There was an awkward pause. In an attempt to be chatty, I asked him what his name was. "Call me M." he answered and I said I would, feeling that here indeed was an element of mystery.

"Come on," said M. and we started the second lap. This was as spectacular as the first. Something seemed to be pulling my feet forward and my head backward and a mirror showed me the unfortunate image of myself executing a sort of Nordic cakewalk while the solicitous M. endeavored to divert my convulsions in the right direction. Once more we paused for breath. In the interval I caught sight of Elise. She was bending forward in the attitude of someone looking for a four-leaf clover and was daintily if uncertainly *walking*, lifting her foot a good six inches with every step. At times her arms, and consequently those of Mr. Kelly flew up in a manner that reminded one of the more animated figures of the Mazurka. This threw them at a perilous angle and I maliciously hoped the orchestra might play "Slide, Kelly Slide." I called to her in what I considered a cheery tone but she gave me in reply only a dirty look.

"Shall we try again?" M. was saying, and once more we lurched forth. This time I managed to steer a straighter course. "You'll do all right," he said not unkindly.

"Oh, do you think so?" I simpered.

"Do you like to dance?" he asked abruptly.

"Yes," I faltered. "Do you?" And feeling that no price was too great to pay, I wondered if he were about to ask me to dinner at the Persian Room. But he only repeated, "Then you'll do all right."

Fired with ambition I started again. By now both of my feet had gone to sleep, and the calves of my legs were only half awake. I was quite numb all over and cheered myself with the thought that no fall could be more painful than the present state of my person. With the courage of despair I set forth at a swifter pace. Unfortunately that unseen force again pulled my head and feet in diametrically opposed directions and once more I was precipitated into the cakewalk, this time with such energy that I found myself going backward in time to the band which was rendering a lively fox trot. M. too seemed to have caught the spirit of the dance, albeit unwillingly, and was backing with me at increasing speed, shouting "Careful!" with as much efficacy as a Paris gendarme calls *"Attention!"* to the traffic.

Faster and faster we flew in a movement that must be difficult for even the most expert. I was aware of people stopping to watch, of flying bits of ice, of Elise's face blanched and horrified; then, in perfect unison, we struck the surface and landed, facing each other tailor-fashion, in the position of two people about to play "Pease Porridge Hot!" Our manoeuvre made a considerable stir and a small band of Merrie Men rushed out, as at the sound of Robin s horn, to our rescue. Firm hands seized and lifted me onto that completely uncontrollable part of my anatomy, my feet, and somebody said "There you are!" as if I didn't know. Unfortunately no bones were broken, so I had to continue my lesson; but Elise, who had witnessed my tumbling act, suddenly remembered she had a date, waved a mitten at me and departed.

The remainder of the time passed uneventfully enough. M., that prince of diplomats, never once referring to our débâcle, patiently steered me, lurching, heaving, now waving my arms as if semaphoring, now bowing as a sovereign to my subjects. I tried the theory of mental images. I thought of Charlotte, of beautiful mad Tartars skimming over the ice of whatever mad Tartars skim over the ice of, of Rear-Admiral Byrd sailing over the Pole; but my power of imagination was defeated by my lack of co-ordination and the reflection of myself in passing mirrors. After half an hour that seemed interminable, M. expressed the opinion that I had done enough for the day. Surely the day had done more than enough for me, and I was only too relieved to be shoved to the edge and deposited on the wooden runway. Thence I made my way in a quaint and somewhat primitive rhythm to the dressing-room.

The colored young lady sighed deeply and unlaced the Iron Maidens. Tales of Northern exposure and frozen members that drop off assailed me and I half expected her to remove my feet with the boots. They appeared, however, still to be attached, though completely paralyzed and bearing across each instep curious markings that made them look like waffles. This interesting design showed plainly through my chiffon hose and lasted most of the day, but I was lucky to have escaped with no further injury.

Since then, Elise and I have returned a few times to the strong arms of M. and Kelly. We have not, however, as yet come into our own—though we have succeeded in coming into everything and everybody in the ice palace. I feel there is too much of the Latin in me to excel in so Nordic a sport, although M. keeps assuring me that if I can dance I ought to do—do what, he doesn't say; and, what's more, I have an idea he is entertaining the petty suspicion that I don't even dance. Elise and I have lately discussed taking up some sport that doesn't hurt so, to re-establish our self-confidence; and, the season being winter, and the month for such things being no nearer than June, we are considering canoeing.

Clap Hands,
Here Comes Charlie

Beryl Bainbridge

Two weeks before Christmas, Angela Bisson gave Mrs Henderson six tickets for the theatre. Mrs Henderson was Angela Bisson's cleaning lady.

"I wanted to avoid giving you money," Angela Bisson told her. "Anybody can give money. Somehow the whole process is so degrading … taking it … giving it. They're reopening the Empire Theatre for a limited season. I wanted to give you a treat. Something you'll always remember."

Mrs Henderson said, "Thank you very much." She had never, when accepting money, felt degraded.

Her husband, Charles Henderson, asked her how much Angela Bisson had tipped her for Christmas.

Mrs Henderson said not much. "In fact," she admitted, "nothing at all. Not in your actual pounds, shillings and pence. We've got tickets for the theatre instead."

"What a discerning woman," cried Charles Henderson. "It's just what we've always needed."

"The kiddies will like it," protested Mrs Henderson. "It's a pantomime. They've never been to a pantomime."

Mrs Henderson's son, Alec, said *Peter Pan* wasn't a pantomime. At least not what his mother understood by the word. Of course, there was a fairy-tale element to the story, dealing as it did with Never-Never land and lost boys, but there was more to it than that. "It's written on several levels," he informed her.

"I've been a lost boy all my life," muttered Charles Henderson, but nobody heard him.

"And I doubt," said Alec, "if our Moira's kiddies will make head nor tail of it. It's full of nannies and coal fires burning in the nursery."

"Don't talk rot," fumed Charles Henderson. "They've seen coal fires on television."

"Shut up, Charlie," said Alec. His father hated being called Charlie.

"Does it have a principal boy?" asked Mrs Henderson, hopefully.

"Yes and no," said Alec. "Not in the sense you mean. Don't expect any singing or any smutty jokes. It's allegorical."

"God Almighty," said Charles Henderson.

When Alec had gone out to attend a Union meeting, Mrs Henderson told her husband he needn't bother to come to the theatre. She wasn't putting up with him and Alec having a pantomime of their own during the course of the evening and spoiling it for everyone else. She'd ask Mrs Rafferty from the floor above to go in his place.

"By heck," shouted Charles Henderson, striking his forehead with the back of his hand, "why didn't I think of that? Perish the thought that our Alec should be the one to be excluded. I'm only the blasted bread-winner." He knew his wife was just mouthing words.

Mrs Rafferty's answer to such an outlandish invitation was a foregone conclusion. She wouldn't give it houseroom. Mrs Rafferty hadn't been out of the building for five years, not since she was bashed over the head coming home from Bingo.

All the same, Charles Henderson was irritated. His wife's attitude, and the caustic remarks addressed to him earlier by Alec brought on another attack of indigestion. It was no use going to his bed and lying flat. He knew from experience that it wouldn't help. In the old days, when they had lived in a proper house, he could have stepped out of the back door and perambulated up and down the yard for a few minutes. Had there been anything so exalted as a back door in this hell-hole, going out of it certainly wouldn't improve his health. Not without a parachute. He couldn't even open the window for a breath of air. This high up there was generally a howling gale blowing in from the river—it would suck the Christmas cards clean off the sideboard. It wasn't normal, he thought, to be perpetually on a par with the clouds. People weren't meant to look out of windows and see nothing but sky, particularly if they weren't looking upwards. God knows how Moira's kiddies managed. They were stuck up in the air over Kirby. When Moira and Alec had been little they'd played in the street—Moira on the front step fiddling with her dolly, Alec on one roller-skate scooting in and out of the lamp-posts. Of course there was no denying that it had been nice at first to own a decent bathroom and have hot water coming out of the tap. After only a few weeks it had become unnecessary to scrub young Alec's neck with his toothbrush; the dirt just floated off on the towel. But there was surely more to life than a clean neck. Their whole existence, once work was over for the day, was lived as though inside the cabin of an aeroplane. And they weren't going anywhere—there wasn't a landing field in sight. Just stars. Thousands of the things, on clear nights, winking away outside the double glazing. It occurred to Charles Henderson that there were too many of them for comfort or for grandeur. It was quality that counted, not quantity.

At the end of the yard of the terraced house in which he had once lived, there had been an outside toilet. Sitting within the evil-smelling little shed, its door swinging on broken hinges, he had sometimes glimpsed one solitary star hung motionless above the city. It had, he felt, given perspective to his situation, his situation in the wider sense—beyond his temporary perch. He was earthbound, mortal, and a million light-years separated him from that pale diamond burning in the sky. One star was all a man needed.

On the night of the outing to the theatre, a bit of a rumpus took place in the lift. It was occasioned by Moira's lad, Wayne, jabbing at all the control buttons and giving his grandmother a turn.

Alec thumped Wayne across the ear and Charles Henderson flared up. "There was no cause to do that," he shouted, though indeed there had been. Wayne was a shocking kiddie for fiddling with things.

"Belt up, Charlie," ordered Alec.

Alec drove them to the Empire theatre in his car. It wasn't a satisfactory arrangement as far as Charles Henderson was concerned but he had no alternative. The buses came and went as they pleased. He was forced to sit next to Alec because he couldn't stand being parked in the back with the children and neither Moira nor Mrs Henderson felt it was safe in the passenger seat. Not with Alec at the wheel. Every time Alec accelerated going round a corner, Charles Henderson was swung against his son's shoulder.

"Get over, can't you?" cried Alec. "Stop leaning on me, Charlie."

When they passed the end of the street in which they had lived a decade ago, Mrs Henderson swivelled in her seat and remarked how changed it was, oh how changed. All those houses knocked down, and for what? Alec said that in his opinion it was good riddance to bad rubbish. The whole area had never been anything but a slum.

"Perhaps you're right, son," said Mrs Henderson. But she was pandering to him.

Charles Henderson was unwise enough to mention times gone by. He was talking to his wife. 'Do you remember all the men playing football in the street after work?"

"I do," she said.

"And using the doorway of the Lune Laundry for a goal-post? It was like living in a village, wasn't it?"

"A village," hooted Alec. "With a tobacco warehouse and a brewery in the middle of it? Some village."

"We hunted foxes in the field behind the public house," reminisced Charles Henderson. "And we went fishing in the canal."

"You did. You were never at home," said Mrs Henderson, without rancour.

"What field?" scoffed Alec. "What canal?"

"There was a time," said Charles Henderson, "when we snared rabbits every Saturday and had them for Sunday dinner. I tell no lies. You might almost say we lived off the land."

"Never-Never land, more like," sneered Alec, and he drove, viciously, the wrong way down a one way street.

When they got to the town centre he made them all get out and stand about in the cold while he manoeuvred the Mini backwards and forwards in the underground car park. He cursed and gesticulated.

"Behave yourself," shouted Charles Henderson, and he strode in front of the bonnet and made a series of authoritative signals. Alec deliberately drove the car straight at him.

"Did you see what that madman did?" Charles Henderson asked his wife. "He ran over my foot."

"You're imagining things," said Mrs Henderson, but when he looked down he saw quite clearly the tread of the tyre imprinted upon the Cherry Blossom shine of his Sunday left shoe.

When the curtain went up, he was beginning to feel the first twinges of his indigestion coming on again. It wasn't to be wondered at all that swopping of seats because Moira had a tall bloke sitting in front of her, and the kiddies tramping back and forth to the toilet, not to mention the carry-on over parking the car. At least he hadn't got Alec sitting next to him. He found the first act of *Peter Pan* a bit of a mystery. It was very old-fashioned and cosy. He supposed they couldn't get a real dog to play the part. Some of the scenery could do with a lick of paint. He didn't actually laugh out loud when Mr Darling complained that nobody coddled him—oh no, why should they, seeing he was only the bread-winner—but he did grunt sardonically; Mrs Henderson nudged him sharply with her elbow. He couldn't for the life of him make out who or what Tinkerbell was, beyond being a sort of glow-worm bobbing up and down on the nursery wall, until Wendy had her hair pulled for wanting Peter to kiss her, and then he more or less guessed Tinkerbell was a female. It was a bit suggestive, all that. And at the end of the first scene when they all flew out of the window, something must have gone wrong with the wires because one of the children never got off the ground. They brought the curtain down fast. Wayne was yawning his head off.

During Acts Two and Three, Charles Henderson dozed. He was aware of loud noises and children screaming in a bloodthirsty fashion. He hoped Wayne wasn't having one of his tantrums. It was confusing for him. He was dreaming he was fishing in the canal for tiddlers and a damn big crocodile crawled up the bank with a clock ticking inside it. Then he heard a drum beating and a voice cried out "To die will be an awfully big adventure." He woke up then with a start. He had a pain in his arm.

In the interval they retired to the bar, Moira and himself and Alec. Mrs Henderson stayed with the kiddies, to give Moira a break. Alec paid for a round of drinks. "Are you enjoying it then, Charlie?" he asked.

"It's a bit loud for me," said Charles Henderson. "But I see what you mean about it being written on different levels."

"You do surprise me," said Alec. "I could have sworn you slept through most of it."

Moira said little Tracy was terrified of the crocodile but she loved the doggie.

"Some doggie," muttered Charles Henderson. "I could smell the moth balls."

"But Wayne thinks it's lovely," said Moira. "He's really engrossed."

"I could tell," Charles Henderson said. "They must have heard him yawning in Birkenhead."

"It's one of his signs," defended Moira. "Yawning. He always yawns when he's engrossed." She herself was enjoying it very much, though she hadn't understood at first what Mr Darling was doing dressed up as Captain Hook.

"It's traditional," Alec told her.

"What are you on about?" asked Charles Henderson. "That pirate chappie was never Mr Darling."

"Yes it was, Dad," said Moira. "I didn't cotton on myself at first, but it was the same man."

"I suppose it saves on wages," Charles Henderson said. Alec explained it was symbolic. The kindly Mr Darling and the brutal Captain Hook were two halves of the same man.

"There wasn't more than a quarter of Mr Darling," cried Charles Henderson, heatedly. "That pirate was waving his cutlass about every time I opened my eyes. I can't see the point of it, can you, Moira?"

Moira said nothing, but her mouth drooped at the corners. She was probably thinking about her husband who had run off and left her with two kiddies and a gas bill for twenty-seven quid.

"The point," said Alec, "is obvious. Mr Darling longs to murder his offspring." He was shouting quite loudly. "Like fathers in real life. They're always out to destroy their children."

"What's up with you?" asked Mrs Henderson, when her husband had returned to his seat.

"That Alec," hissed Charles Henderson. "He talks a load of codswallop. I'd like to throttle him."

During Act Four Charles Henderson asked his wife for a peppermint. His indigestion was fearsome. Mrs Henderson told him to shush. She too seemed engrossed in the pantomime. Wayne was sitting bolt upright. Charles Henderson tried to concentrate. He heard some words but not others. The lost boys were going back to their Mums, that much he gathered. Somebody called Tiger Lily had come into it. And Indians were beating tom-toms. His heart was beating so loudly that it was a wonder Alec didn't fly off the handle and order him to keep quiet. Wendy had flown off with the boys, jerkily, and Peter was asleep. It was odd how it was all to do with flying. That Tinkerbell person was flashing about among the cloth trees. He had the curious delusion that if he stood up on his seat, he too might soar up into the gallery. It was a daft notion because when he tried to shift his legs they were as heavy as lead. Mrs Darling would be pleased to see the kiddies again. She must have gone through hell. He remembered the time Alec had come home half an hour late from the Cubs—the length of those minutes, the depth of that fear. It didn't matter what his feelings had been towards Alec for the last ten years. He didn't think you were supposed to feel much for grown-up children. He had loved little Alec, now a lost boy, and that was enough.

Something dramatic was happening on stage. Peter had woken up and was having a disjointed conversation with Tinkerbell, something to do with cough mixture and poison. *Tink, you have drunk my medicine … it was poisoned and you drank it to save my life … Tink dear, are you dying? …* The tiny star that was Tinkerbell began to flicker. Charles Henderson could hear somebody sobbing. He craned sideways to look down the row and was astonished to see that his grandson was wiping at his eyes with the back of his sleeve. Fancy Wayne, a lad who last year had been caught dangling a hamster on a piece of string from a window on the fourteenth floor of the flats, crying about a light going out. Peter Pan was advancing towards the audience, his arms flung wide. *Her voice is so low I can hardly hear what she is saying. She says … she says she thinks she could get well again if children believed in fairies. Say quick that you believe. If you believe, clap your hands. Clap your hands and Tinkerbell will live.*

At first the clapping was muted, apologetic. Tinkerbell was reduced to a dying spark quivering on the dusty floorboards of the stage. Charles Henderson's own hands were clasped to his chest. There was a pain inside him as though somebody had slung a hook through his heart. The clapping increased in volume. The feeble Tinkerbell began to glow. She sailed triumphantly up the trunk of a painted tree. She grew so dazzling that Charles Henderson was blinded. She blazed above him in the skies of Never-Never land.

"Help me," he said, using his last breath.

"Shut up, Charlie," shouted Mrs Henderson, and she clapped and clapped until the palms of her hands were stinging.

The Pantomime

STELLA MARGETSON

The boy was fascinated. He didn't mind what she asked him to do. He fixed up the footlights, each lamp which he had borrowed from his mother's store cupboard, shaded by an empty canned meat tin thrown out of the officers' mess. He showed her the way it worked and he was rather proud when she admired the arrangement, standing and staring at her with a smile in his luminous dark eyes, his big capable hands hanging down from the wrinkled sleeves of a jacket he had grown out of.

"It would have been better still," he said in his cracked, adolescent voice, "if I'd had more time. I'd have fixed up limelight with coloured slides."

"But it's marvellous," she assured him. "You are a clever boy. I shall call you the assistant stage-manager."

"Thanks," he said seriously. "I like that." He still couldn't quite believe in this new, exciting experience of being allowed to help with a real production. It had come so suddenly, from his first meeting with her by the edge of the desolate harbour beyond Saxham, when she had stopped to ask him the way. One thing leading to another, she had found out where he lived and had told him she was staying in New Saxham to be near her husband and was getting up a pantomime among the men for New Year's Eve. Would he like to help her? Yes, he would. … He hadn't any other idea in his head now.

She smiled at him. "What are we going to do for scenery?"

"I think I could fetch some things from home—at least, if I can persuade mother to lend them. I've got that beard you wanted me to make." Diving into his pockets, he brought out a penknife, a sticky piece of toffee, three beech nuts and a piece of cotton-wool. "I stuck it on to some gauze," he said, smoothing it carefully. "To make it firmer. You can easily cut it if it isn't the right shape."

She laughed. "It looks perfect. Where's Tom? T–o–m!" she called. "Come and try your beaver."

"'Arf a mo', Missus, we're 'avin' trouble with this 'ere fairy queen —'is bust's come to grief."

"Blimey, it's slipped down to me navel!" the fairy queen expostulated. "'Oo believes in fairies? I'm blowed if I do!"

He took a skip and a dance on to the stage, holding the recalcitrant bust round his waist, the trousers of his battle dress emerging from a pink tulle skirt.

She laughed so much she could hardly speak. "If you go on like that, George, we shall never get the rehearsal going! Let me look, I shall have to sew your bosom into the dress. You can leave it off for the moment, we must go through the scene."

The big gunner scratched his head. "Course, I'd rather not 'ave it at all—I mean with ladies in the audience," he said bashfully.

"Oh, you needn't worry about the ladies," she told him. "They'll laugh."

"Well, I don't know—it's a bit of an exhibition."

"Nonsense! You do it grandly. Besides don't you count me a lady?"

"Ah, you're different, Missus—meanin' no offence, of course." She was such a sport, so friendly and such a gay duck, they all loved her and she knew it, he guessed. She didn't half make things hum and she never gave herself airs, not like some officers' wives. The things she did for them! Why, she was like a mother to the battery— only she was a little thing with a pretty figure and dainty feet—she had been a dancer—and you couldn't very well call a girl like that mother. More like a sweetheart—though none of them would ever presume to touch a hair of her head, or let anyone else either. "Ay, you're different," he said again.

"I know—" she turned to the boy— "We needn't have any scenery. We can have a notice: Scene I, The Barrack Square; Scene II, The Cookhouse; Scene III, The Palais de Danse, and so on. Could you paint a notice for me, do you think?"

"Yes." He was immensely relieved because he would not have to ask his mother to lend anything.

"Have you got a bit of wood or a bit of cardboard?" she said.

"Yes, I've got the very thing."

He ran home, mounting the stairs three at a time to his attic room. Under the accumulated rubbish that he loved and played with alone, he found the dart-board and ripped off the back. It had a lot of holes in it where he had thrown wide of the mark, but he didn't think it would matter. It was a treasured possession, but that didn't matter either. It was the very thing for her.

He worked frantically to get it off without splitting the wood. Then he rummaged in the cupboard where he kept his painting things, choosing a bold colour which he thought she would like.

But just as he was coming downstairs with all the things under his arm, his mother stopped him. She was a gaunt unhappy looking woman, painfully reserved.

"What are you doing?" she demanded.

"Taking sone things over for the pantomime."

"What things?"

"Some things we want for the scenery."

"None of my things, I hope."

"Oh, no!" For a moment he thought she was going to begin again about the electric light bulbs he had borrowed, but she said nothing and he ran back to the recreation hut.

She was putting the "principal girl" through his paces, a lanky gunner wearing a W.A.A.F. uniform, trying to make him keep time with the pianist. "Come on, work it up, Bill," she sang.

"Only you, only you—

Sing it as if you mean it—

I've never had a love,
I've never had a boy,
Only you, only you. ...

Come on Peter, sing it *to* her, that's it—

I've never had a girl,
Only you, only you. ..."

The boy stood watching her, silent and happy. She was a dark silhouette, a figure moving to the rhythm of the tune; and the men on the stage were following her direction, beads of sweat glistening on their faces. It was hot inside the hut, the oil-stove gave off a reeky odour that mingled with the smell of khaki and stale cigarette smoke. The boy felt warm and comfortable, like he felt sometimes in his attic on a winter's evening—only this was better, so much better because he wasn't alone any longer.

He smiled with shy eagerness, not interrupting her until she came to the end of the duet. "I've got this board—will it do?"

"Yes, rather."

"I've got some paints too. A bright sort of emerald green—look."

"Oh, that's lovely!" she exclaimed.

"I'll do it now, shall I?"

He settled down at the back of the hut, while the rehearsal went on. The fairy queen couldn't remember his lines, but she didn't lose her patience; she laughed, coaxing him, while the pianist banged away on the old piano.

"Now, once more," she said. "Here's your cue:

They don't give me a chance
To get a bit of skirt. ...

Now—"

He lumbered on to the stage and pirouetted in his army boots, waving a lavatory brush as a wand.

"I am the Fairy Queen,
If you please to hear me," he warbled.
"A bit of a has been,

If you knew really.
The boys I've had under wing—
Strewth, it would make you start!
Oh, you've no idea what a thing
It is to be a fairy tart!"

"Another pirouette," she said. "Your intonation is gorgeous, keep it up—"

"But soft—what see I here?
A young man all un'appy?
I'll whisper Whisky in his ear :
What ails thee, lad? Make it snappy...."

The boy worked steadily at the notice board. Scene I. THE BARRACK SQUARE. Scene II. THE COOKHOUSE. Scene III. THE PALLEY DE DANCE. ... He drew the letters carefully and painted them, glancing up when her husband came in.

"Hullo, Joe—have you seen Pam?" the lieutenant said.

The boy gazed at him, worshipping his manliness. "She's up there," he answered.

"Hey, I say—" the lieutenant was about to point out the incorrect spelling of Palais de Danse, but looking at the boy, refrained. Pam said he was a sensitive kid; she thought he had a pretty tough time living alone with that curious mother of his, who didn't appear to give a damn for him, except to abuse him occasionally. And he was a nice lad with a serious kind of enthusiasm, the imaginative type—

She came up to them. "You've just missed the fairy queen, Stephen. He'll make your sides ache."

"Well, thank God you planned the show for New Year's Eve," he said. "I've just had a notice putting forward the date—I shall have to go on New Year's Day. Isn't it damnable?"

The boy listened. Stephen was going to Wales on a special course and she was going home when he left, going back to Gloucestershire—but this had been a long way off, he hadn't considered it.

"What a nuisance, darling. Never mind, we'll get the pantomime done," she said. "And it is going to be funny, isn't it, Joe?"

When she turned like that and looked at him, the boy felt a wave of light flooding him, too strong, too dazzling, too exciting— but gentle also, and compassionate.

"Yes," he said. "It is going to be fun."

❄

The recreation hut was packed for the performance. A roaring, expectant crowd of men, ready to laugh at anything; the Major and the Captain, and a few of the local residents, like the boy's mother, who scarcely laughed at all, the lady from next door and the two old girls from the end of the road, who hadn't seen a show for years. The bawdier it became, the better the two old ladies liked it and the more they laughed. The Major had quite a shock when he looked round to see who was laughing so hilariously; tears were pouring down their cheeks, they hadn't enjoyed anything so much since their youth, long ago.

She was working hard behind the scenes to make the show a success: fitting the fairy queen into his false bosom, fixing blonde crepe hair to the "principal girl's" cap, urging Peter not to be frightened of the duet. ... The boy, who was wearing his best suit of a dark cloth, ran errands for her between the stage and the audience. He worked the lights and retrieved the lavatory brush when the Fairy Queen with a lusty wave, threw it at the Major's head. He was angry and sore about the notice. George had told him the spelling was wrong. "Blimey, you ain't never 'eard of a Palais de Danse!" he said, laughing at him. "Or bin to one neither, it seems. ..." making him feel ashamed. But she said it didn't matter, it was more amusing that way; she thought he had done it purposely. Then George gave her a wink and made a gesture which the boy couldn't interpret, although he felt certain the big gunner was making fun of him.

From his perch by the light switch, he could see her, half hidden behind the curtains with the script in her hand. It was the big scene, leading to the duet. The pianist thumped on the worn out piano and Bill sang the first verse with falsetto gusto, then Peter came in:

> "Only you, only you,
> I've never had a love,
> I've never had a girl. ..."

The audience roared with laughter when Bill powdered his nose. But the boy suddenly put his head in his hands.

> "Only you, only you. ..."

The realisation was terrible. Lightnings and thunders shook him from head to foot and left him pale and shivering. Then he glowed with a great warmth, a love bigger than himself penetrating all his seriousness, embracing all the past and wiping away its loneliness. He wanted to lie down so that she could walk over him. He wanted to give, to go on giving, giving. ...

The audience yelled for an encore. And now Peter seemed to be singing differently, all his heart in the song—

"Lights!" someone shouted. And the boy looked up, in time to see her eyes on him and to touch the switch at his elbow.

❄

The boy had grown up. He felt different. When she had taken his hand at the end of the show to drag him in front of the footlights as her assistant stage-manager, he had felt strong and resourceful. But now, in his attic room, the show was over; he had put the lamps back in his mother's store-cupboard, there was nothing left to do. To-morrow, early in the morning, she was going away.

Out in the road, some of the men were still singing. To-morrow the New Year began; to-morrow she was going away. He had promised to go and say good-bye to her. But he couldn't go now; he couldn't ever see her again now that he knew he loved her.

He thought he would make something and leave it for her before she was up. He was clever with his fingers; he could make almost anything, only he didn't know what to make. He emptied the pockets of his old jacket again, staring at the beech-nuts and the penknife and the sticky piece of toffee. There wasn't much inspiration in them and he felt a terrible emptiness; he had outgrown the things lying on the table, he couldn't even remember why he had kept the beech-nuts. To-morrow, early in the morning, she was going away.

He pulled some things out of the cupboard, slowly this time, trying to make up his mind what to make. Then he sat down, sketching some animals at random—a dog, a cat, a giraffe, some birds flying, and a rabbit. He remembered the gulls they had seen flying over the desolate, disused harbour beyond Saxham. She said she loved watching them, they were so beautiful. He hadn't tried making a sea-gull before. It took him a long time, first to draw it on the wood, then to carve it out and paint it. When he had finished, he went to bed, long after midnight.

In the morning, he wasn't very pleased with the sea-gull; it looked a bit clumsy. But he couldn't do anything about it. He wrote a little note: "With love from Joe," and hurried round to the house where she was staying. It was dark still, the sky a dark electric blue merging into a translucent green towards the east, the morning late, reluctant to dawn after the black-out. He shivered. The bell rang through the house and he waited.

She was in the hall, tying labels on her luggage.

"Joe! My dear, come in. Have you got over the show?"

"Oh, I didn't want to see you," he began. "I mean—I thought I'd be too early." He hesitated. "I've brought something for you, I hope you'll like it."

He was going away, but she called him back.

"Did you make this?"

He nodded, staring at her.

"Did you make it specially for me?"

"Yes."

"How sweet of you. I shall keep it."

Then he knew she understood, even before she took his head in her hands and kissed him.

"That for the New Year," she said. "Good-bye, Joe. Be happy."

When he walked away, the sky had changed and the sun was rising beyond Saxham.

On Leavin' Notes

ALICE CHILDRESS

❄

Good evenin', Marge. I just stopped by to say "Hey" … No thank you darlin', I do not care for any turkey hash, and I don't like turkey soup or creamed turkey either. Child, there's nothin' as sickenin' as a "hanging around" turkey.

Well girl, I done come up with my New Year's resolution. … That's right, I made just one, and that is this: NOBODY THAT I DO DAYSWORK FOR SHALL LEAVE ME ANY NOTES … You know what I mean. Whenever these women are going to be out when you come to work, they will leave you a note tellin' you about a few extra things to do. They ask you things in them notes that they wouldn't dast ask you to your face.

When I opened the door this morning I found a note from Mrs. R. It was neatly pinned to three cotton housecoats. "Dear Mildred," it read, "please take these home, wash and iron them, and bring them in tomorrow. Here is an extra dollar for you. …" And at the bottom of the note a dollar was pinned.

Now Marge, there is a laundry right up on her corner and they charges seventy-five cents for housecoats. … Wait a minute, honey, just let me tell it now. … I hung around until she got home … Oh, but I did! And she was most surprised to see the housecoats and me still there. "Mildred," says she, "did you see my note?"

"Yes," I replied, "and I cannot do those housecoats for no dollar."

"Why," she says, "how much do you want?"

I give her a sparing smile and says, "Seventy-five cents apiece, the same as the laundry."

"Oh," she says, "well it looks as though I can't use you. ..."

"Indeed you can't," I say, "'cause furthermore I am not going to let you."

"Let's not get upset," she adds. "I only meant I won't need you for the laundry."

"I am not upset, Mrs. R.," I says, "but in the future, please don't leave me any notes making requests outside of our agreement. ..." And do you know, THAT was THAT. ... No, Marge ... I did not pop my fingers at her when I said it. There's no need to overdo the thing!

Copyright Notices

✳

'The Turkey Season' by Alice Munro, taken from *The Moons of Jupiter*, published by Vintage. Copyright © Alice Munro 1982. Reprinted with permission of The Random House Group Limited.

'This Year It Will Be Different' by Maeve Binchy, © 1996. Published in *This Year It Will Be Different* by the Orion Publishing Group, 2008. Reproduced with permission of the Licensor through PLSclear.

'The Christmas Pageant' by Barbara Robinson, © 1968. Reproduced with permission of Robinson Literary Works, LLC.

''Twas the Night Before Christmas' by Kate Nivison, © 1989.

'Christmas Fugue' from *The Complete Short Stories* by Muriel Spark (Canongate), © Copyright Administration Limited, reproduced by permission of David Higham Associates.

'The Little Christmas Tree' by Stella Gibbons. Reproduced with permission of Curtis Brown Group Ltd, London, on behalf of the Beneficiaries of the Estate of Stella Gibbons. Copyright © Stella Gibbons, 1940.

'The Christmas Present' by Richmal Crompton, © 1922 Edward Ashbee and Catherine Massey. Reproduced by permission of United Agents.

'On Skating' from *Excuse It, Please!* by Cornelia Otis Skinner, © 1936.

'Clap Hands, Here Comes Charlie' from *Mum and Mr Armitage* by Beryl Bainbridge (Gerald Duckworth & Co Ltd, 1985). Reproduced with permission of Johnson & Alcock Ltd.

'Pantomime' from *Flood Tide and Other Stories* by Stella Margetson, © 1943.

'On Leavin' Notes' by Alice Childress. Copyright 1956. Copyright renewed 1984. Used by permission of SLD Associates LLC, sarah.douglas@sldassociatesllc.com

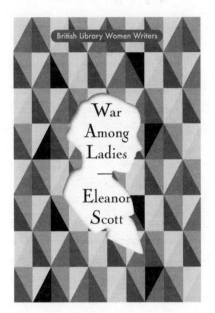

"There is something appalling in this warfare, silent, secret and unrelenting, that is waged by polite women with smiling faces and gentle manner, against one another."

The staffroom at Besley High School for girls simmers with hushed resentments. In a graduation system whereby the failure in one subject means that a pupil fails overall, the shortcomings of just one teacher threatens them all. Viola Kennedy, a newly arrived young teacher full of optimism and ideas, gets caught up in the politics and scheming. This is a quietly devastating novel about the realities of life for single working women in the 1920s and the systems that failed them.

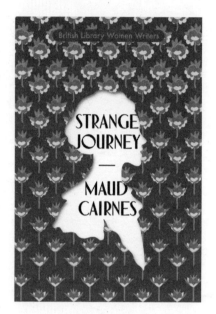

"Oh well, if you don't want to hear my news—" He loosed my arm, and I hurried from the room, reflecting that I had offended two husbands in one day, a record for any woman.

In this body swap comedy from the 1930s, the minds of two strangers, Lady Elizabeth and Polly Wilkinson, switch places—randomly and without warning—with alarming and hilarious results. With wry observations on class, behaviour and relationships, as both attempt to navigate the different social settings and awkward personal situations they suddenly find themselves thrust into, the two women eventually learn to control their 'gift' and use it to their advantage.